MURDER IN WHISTLER

A Northwest Cozy Mystery - Book 2

BY

DIANNE HARMAN

CONTENTS

ACKNOWLEDGMENTS

Last summer, when I visited Whistler, British Columbia, I soon realized that the setting was perfect for a book. The golf courses, the scenery, and the charming village, all deserved to have something written about them. Since I was starting a new series about the Pacific Northwest, Whistler fit in perfectly. I just wasn't sure who, how, or when someone was going to get murdered. As the book took form, so, too, did the characters and the story line. While the characters came out of my imagination, the setting did not. The Fairmont is a wonderful hotel, as is everything else in Whistler. If you've not visited this little jewel of a town in spectacular British Columbia, I strongly urge you to put it on your bucket list!

As always, thanks to the two men who make all of my books possible – Vivek and Tom.

To Vivek: I rely on this man to design my book covers, handle the technical side of publishing my books, and give me wise counsel, which he always does. Thanks!

To Tom: I rely on him to free me from the day to day household chores so I can do what I love – write. Thanks for handling everything so competently! Our home operates seamlessly because of you, and for that I'm truly appreciative.

And last, but certainly not least, To You, My Readers: I so appreciate your support by borrowing my books on Kindle Unlimited and/or buying them. It makes me feel very special when you take the time to write and tell me how much you enjoy a book or a character, or even ask me when the next one will be published. Thank you!

Win FREE Paperbacks every week!

Go to www.dianneharman.com/freepaperback.html and get your FREE copies of Dianne's books and favorite recipes immediately by signing up for her newsletter.

Once you've signed up for her newsletter you're eligible to win three paperbacks. One lucky winner is picked every week. Hurry before the offer ends!

PROLOGUE

Johnny Roberts stood on the balcony of his penthouse suite at the Fairmont Chateau Whistler Hotel and stretched out his tanned arms. An attractive man in his early fifties, his shiny bald head was just as brown as his weather-beaten limbs. He filled his lungs with the cool, fresh, mountain air for which Whistler, British Columbia, is so well known, and exhaled. Even if you were fifty feet away, you always knew it was Johnny because of two things, his bushy white mustache and the large Rolex Submariner blue dial watch that he wore on his wrist.

The majestic ski slopes of Blackcomb mountain lay before him, the dark rock face and acres of deep green pines still untouched by snow. The September morning was cool, and the sun was just starting to peek over the horizon. Johnny was an early riser, even when he was on vacation. He'd already completed his workout in the hotel's fitness center and was showered and dressed, ready for his daily 7:00 a.m. telephone conference with his assistant, Dorothy. She ran his life like clockwork, and he didn't see any reason to change the routine just because he was in British Columbia on a three-day golf trip.

"Gotta be Dorothy, right on time," Johnny said to himself with a smile as the expected call came through on his cell phone. He moved inside to the suite and sat down at the large hand-crafted wooden executive desk. His laptop was open, and he saw that Dorothy had already synched his calendar.

"Good morning Mr. Roberts."

Johnny liked how Dorothy Stettner still called him Mr. Roberts even though she'd been working for him at his Mercedes dealership in Seattle, J.R. Mercedes, for twenty-five years. Theirs was a working relationship built on mutual respect. Johnny often thought the young people who applied for a job at his dealership these days not only lacked manners, but had an attitude of entitlement. They didn't seem to have any respect for the older generation, which didn't sit well with him. He'd debated the issue with his wife, Cassie, who'd laughed and told him he was just out of touch with today's younger generation.

"Hi, Dorothy," Johnny said, checking his calendar as he looked at his computer. He paused. "Dorothy, I know I have a breakfast meeting at 7:30. this morning, but I sure wish I could go directly to the golf course."

"I understand. Would you like me to reschedule it?"

Johnny thought about it for a few seconds. He leaned back in the chair and stared at the wall. "No, never mind. I better take the meeting, but hopefully it will be quick." He relaxed and looked back at the computer screen. "Would you run the golf arrangements by me again? Actually, that's what's the most important to me."

Johnny listened as Dorothy rattled off the golfing agenda for the next three days. As president of the Men's Golf Excursions group for the Island View Golf Club, it was important to Johnny that everything connected with the group's golf outing to Whistler went without a hitch. With Dorothy's help, he'd been planning this trip for months. His meticulous attention to detail in every area, right down to the golf balls to be laid on the guests' pillows at night, was evidence that he wanted this weekend to be special.

"Of course, Mr. Roberts," Dorothy said. "Everything has been triple-checked and confirmed. Today, Saturday, you're playing at the

Fairmont Chateau Whistler Golf Course adjacent to your hotel. The first tee time is booked for 9:00 a.m. and the golf pro for the course will be expecting you any time after 8:00."

Johnny nodded with approval. No matter how much he trusted Dorothy, she knew he'd want to get there early to check on everything for himself.

"Sunday's round is at Whistler Golf Club," Dorothy continued, "and on Monday you'll be playing at the Nicklaus North Golf Course. Then it's back to the Fairmont on Monday night for the awards dinner. I've booked a private dining room and a sommelier for your group, the full works. The concierge has all the details of the menu I've selected."

"Excellent, Dorothy." Johnny glanced at his Rolex. "As always, thanks. I was going to call Cassie, but it looks like I don't have time before breakfast. I'll call you from the golf course in an hour or so. Did the golf club wedges arrive safely?" The Ping Glide chipping wedges had been specially ordered as gifts for the twenty members of the golf club on the golf excursion, and Johnny had confirmed the day before that they had been sent by FedEx directly to the Fairmont.

"Yes, I called the concierge, and they've arrived. You'll need to check the engravings though."

Each person's wedge had been individually engraved with his name. A misspelling was just the sort of thing that could go wrong, and Dorothy knew that Johnny would want to go over each one personally.

"Got it. Thanks Dorothy, I'll talk to you later." Johnny ended the call and stood up. He checked his reflection in the full-length mirror. Dressed in beige golf slacks and a pink short-sleeve polo shirt with a navy sleeveless sweater embroidered with the Island View Golf Club logo, he looked younger than his years. Hard work and a healthy lifestyle were Johnny's secrets to success. He knew he'd been guilty of too much work and not enough play in the past, but he was making an effort to change that. Life was good.

As he was getting ready to leave, there was a knock on the door and a voice said, "It's Josh with room service."

Johnny opened the door and said to the young man who stood in front of the door in the hallway, "I'm sorry, but there must be a mistake. I didn't order anything from room service."

Josh responded, "Every morning the Fairmont provides a complementary pot of coffee to the guests who stay in the penthouse suite. It's just part of our service." He walked into the room and set the tray holding a pot of coffee, a cup, and a white linen napkin on the desk. He turned around and faced Johnny, "Have a good day, sir."

Johnny reached for his wallet and gave the young man a tip as he left the suite. When he closed the door, the thought went through Johnny's mind that Josh certainly didn't seem to be as high caliber as the rest of the Whistler staff he'd encountered. Having hired hundreds of employees over the years, he was a stickler for appropriate appearances. Josh's jacket didn't fit properly, his hair didn't look like it had been washed for several days, and he had a scar running from the corner of his eye to his mouth. Johnny thought he wouldn't want his wife or his daughter opening their hotel door to a man who looked like that.

He took several swallows of the coffee as he grabbed his wallet and phone before bounding downstairs for breakfast. He never rode the elevator, and always took the stairs, two at a time. It was a habit that had delighted both of his children when they were younger, and embarrassed them now that they were adults. However, Johnny was his own man and what they thought didn't concern him in the slightest.

*****

As arranged by Dorothy, the hotel valet service was waiting for Johnny after he finished his breakfast meeting to take him the short distance to the Fairmont Golf Course. Some of the men from the Island View Golf Club were already there, and Johnny greeted them with his usual friendly exuberance and a handshake. "Great morning guys, it's going to be a super day to hit them long and straight."

The men nodded and smiled. In general, the camaraderie among the group was good, and Johnny got along well with them, having been a member of the Island View Golf Club for many years.

After exchanging pleasantries, Johnny nodded toward the line of waiting golf carts. "I've got a few things I need to check out at the first tee box. There might be a little surprise for all of you when you get there, so don't be late." He winked and jumped in a golf cart.

The cart shook as Johnny put his foot to the floor and raced the small vehicle along the cart path leading to the first tee. He knew he was driving the golf cart too fast, but Johnny Roberts never shied away from controversy, and he hadn't gotten to where he was without ruffling a few feathers. Being the owner of a prestigious car dealership, Johnny didn't drive anywhere slowly. He had far too much to do and too little time to do it. He liked to feel the wind in his face and adrenalin pumping through his veins as he raced his Mercedes 300C convertible around town. If that meant a speeding ticket now and then, it came with the territory.

All twenty of the shiny wedges he had special ordered were lined up in a rack on the edge of the first tee box. The sun, rising against the shadow of the mountain, glinted against the shining metal club heads. Johnny parked his golf cart and strode across the grass to inspect the clubs. He lifted one from the rack, grasping it by the pristine leather grip and turned it around to inspect the engraving. A broad grin crossed his face as he reached into his pocket for his cell phone.

"Dorothy, you've done it again. The clubs are superb," Johnny said, picking up another wedge which was just as perfect as the first. "Great start to the tournament, thank you. I can tell it's going to be a good one." A sudden pain in his stomach caused him to bend over and support himself by leaning his arm on his knee.

"No problem, Mr. Roberts. I hope you play to your handicap or better. Have a fantastic day."

"I sure will. I'm just getting ready to call Cassie. Bye, Dorothy." Johnny ended the call and grimaced as another wave of stomach pain overtook him, even more severe than the first. This time he doubled completely over. He waited for it to pass, and when he straightened up he had to wipe away the clammy sweat that had broken out on his forehead. He started to walk back to his golf cart, but his legs were weak and shaky. He knew he had to get to medical help as fast as possible. He managed to take just two steps before he was stopped again by another wave of nausea. With a mounting sense of fear, he realized he wasn't going to be able to get to his cart.

He keeled over and fell to the ground with a thump that no one was around to hear. The Ping Glide wedge and the cell phone he'd been holding in his hand lay on the grass beside him, and the metal of Johnny's Rolex Submariner watch glimmered brightly in the morning sunlight.

CHAPTER ONE

"That was delicious, but I can't eat another bite," DeeDee Wilson said as she pushed the crumb-covered plate across the coffee shop table, out of arm's reach. A small piece of chocolate cake remained on the plate. "Tammy, you know my weakness is chocolate cake. I suppose I should just walk around town with a sign pinned on my back that says, 'My name's DeeDee Wilson. Will talk for chocolate cake.'"

Tammy Lynn smiled from across the table. "Indeed, I do know about your weakness, but tell me, is a piece of chocolate cake what it takes to catch up with you these days? You're so busy I never see you."

The two women were sitting in Buddy's Dog Friendly Cafe, the restaurant owned by Tammy and located on Bainbridge Island in Washington. Even though Buddy's welcomed dogs, DeeDee had left her dog, Balto, at her nearby home.

"I'm so sorry," DeeDee said, before taking a sip of her cappuccino. "Things have been so crazy with work. I didn't want to turn down any clients, so I've been taking every booking that comes my way."

Tammy nodded. "That's understandable, and I've been hearing great reports about Deelish, your new catering business. I'm so happy it's going well for you, but you need some time to yourself as well, you know?"

"You're right," DeeDee said. She'd started her catering business, just a few months earlier in May, after moving to Bainbridge Island following her divorce. Tammy had encouraged DeeDee to start the business when she'd been unsure whether or not she could do it. Tammy also had helped her out by sending some catering bookings her way. Things had gotten off to a shaky start, due to a murder that occurred at the first Deelish dinner party event she catered, but the business had found its feet and was growing steadily by word of mouth.

"I'm going to have to think about taking on a part-time assistant to take over the paperwork and bookings, and an assistant could also manage the social media accounts and marketing." DeeDee giggled, "As hard as I try, I've never really gotten the hang of that Pinterest thing."

A waitress stopped by the table. "You didn't finish your cake, DeeDee," said the young woman, pointing down at the plate. She looked sternly at DeeDee and then grinned. Susie, who worked part-time at Tammy's cafe, was also on DeeDee's payroll, helping her as a server at Deelish catering events.

DeeDee looked up at the young woman. "Hi, Susie. I'm trying to be good, and that really was a giant slice of Chocolate Tiramisu Cake. We're off to Whistler in British Columbia tomorrow morning, to see my sister Roz, so I think it may be a long indulgence-filled three days. Or at least, I hope so."

Tammy and Susie were both staring at DeeDee, waiting for more information. DeeDee's face flushed. "Um, I think we need more details," Tammy said, leaning in with a conspiratorial look on her face. "So just exactly who are you going to Whistler with? Anyone we know?"

DeeDee shrugged. She knew where this conversation was going, so she decided to play along. "Well, if you're talking about the number one guy in my life, who has beautiful thick hair, has one brown eye and one blue, constantly seeks food, leaps around on all fours, likes to chew on a squeaking rabbit toy, and loves me unconditionally, then I guess Balto is definitely someone you know, don't you?"

Tammy's eyes widened. She winked up at Susie. "I knew it. So, Jake's going too? I remember you guys talked about taking a trip together a while ago, but I never heard anything more about it. Seems like you two are getting along well."

Some customers sat down at a nearby table, and Susie reached for an order book and pen from her apron pocket. "I want to hear all about this later," Susie said smiling as she walked off to greet the arriving customers.

"And I want to hear all about it now," Tammy said.

DeeDee had been dating Jake Rodgers since she'd bought Balto from him when she moved to Bainbridge Island. The fact that he'd saved her life not long after that was something that had brought them closer together. Knowing that Jake was watching out for her meant a lot to DeeDee, especially after having just come out of a long marriage and a messy divorce. When her ex-husband had left her for a younger woman, DeeDee's confidence had been badly shaken. She hadn't been looking for another relationship, but when she met Jake, things just seemed to fall naturally into place. Those big blue eyes of his had started it, and his calm, quiet strength certainly had helped things along.

DeeDee shrugged. "There's not much to tell. It's all good, I guess, but we don't have much time to see each other. Jake's busy with his private investigator cases, so we try to get together when we can. I'm really looking forward to a few days away, and as much as I love Bainbridge Island, a change of scenery will be good for both of us. Not to mention no cooking for three days! Roz says she has everything covered, although I think Clark is the cook in that relationship."

"Are you driving up in Jake's motorhome?"

DeeDee shook her head. "No, that was the original plan, but Roz insisted we stay with Clark and her. She wants us to see the alpine lodge style home they've rented, which does sound amazing. They were in temporary accommodations when they first got there, and they just moved into this new place. We're going to take my SUV, and Jake will drive. It only takes about three hours to drive up there, but we plan on taking our time and stopping off along the way."

"How are things with Roz? I bet you miss her."

DeeDee had been surprised when her younger sister, thirty-nine-year-old Roz, had moved to Whistler with her boyfriend Clark. Clark, an engineer, was the project manager for a new ski lift which was being built at Whistler. Since the Whistler Blackcomb ski resort had been named as the best ski resort in North America for the last three years, it was badly needed. It was likely Roz and Clark would be there for at least six months, if not longer.

"Sure, I miss her," DeeDee said, "but we talk all the time, and I'm really happy for her. Clark's a great guy and from what she's said on the phone, it sounds like she made the right decision." DeeDee hesitated before continuing. "I'll be able to find out more when I see her. I have a feeling Roz isn't telling me everything."

DeeDee was secretly worried about Roz, but she didn't want to voice her fears to Tammy. She just had a feeling there was something up with Roz, and she was determined to find out what it was on this trip.

"That's good," Tammy said, eyeing her friend with concern. DeeDee looked up at Tammy and realized that even though the two women had not been friends for very long, Tammy probably knew that DeeDee wasn't telling her the whole story. DeeDee was grateful Tammy respected her enough not to pursue the matter.

Tammy leaned across the table and squeezed DeeDee's hand. "You know I'm here any time you want to talk. Just enjoy the next few days and get some R&R. Drop by with Balto when you guys get back and let me know how it went. By the way, are you going to Leo's 'Ice Cream Dream' next week?"

DeeDee brightened up. "Of course! Leo made me promise not to miss it. No one in their right mind would pass on a free gelato from DaVinci's, the best ice cream parlor on the island."

"Best in the world, according to Leo," Tammy said. "He does this special party for his customers every year at the end of the summer season, before closing his shop for a few weeks. Then he's off to Italy for his annual trip to see his mother. Leo's old, so his mother must be ancient." Tammy sighed, and her face turned serious. "It's hard to think that one of these years he won't have a mother to go back to."

DeeDee felt her heart fill with affection for the old Italian man loved by everyone in the small town she now called home. She was so happy to have met many of the local island residents, and grateful for how they had welcomed her into their community. She stood up, smoothed her skirt, and smiled at her friend. "I better get home and pack a few things for the trip. See you when I get back." She reached in her purse for her wallet, but Tammy waved her away.

"This one's on me. See you and Balto next week at DaVinci's. Have a great time. And I want ALL the details when you get back," she said grinning.

"Okay, I promise," DeeDee said as she started to make her way out. "Although I don't think there will be much to report. After all, there isn't much that could happen on a quiet weekend trip to Whistler."

*****

Balto was waiting on the front porch for DeeDee when she arrived home. He ran down the steps to meet her as she got out of her car, his leash in his mouth.

DeeDee laughed, closed the car door, and bent down to rub his black and white furry coat. "All right, Balto. We'll go out soon. I just need to organize a few things, and then we can have a nice evening together. How about a walk and then dinner? But it needs to be an early night, since we're going away tomorrow morning."

Balto moved his head in what may have been a nod, but DeeDee suspected it was Balto's version of a doggy shrug.

DeeDee opened the mailbox and took out the mail. When she was back inside the house she put the mail and her car keys on the table in the hallway. She noticed that the light was flashing on her answering machine, but she decided to let it go. *I'm on vacation*, she thought to herself. *Work can wait for a few days.*

DeeDee made her way upstairs to her bedroom and stared at the mountain of clothes on the bed. She'd started pulling things out of the closet earlier, trying to decide what to take on the trip, but she got overwhelmed and decided instead to go out and run some errands.

Hmm, big mistake, DeeDee, she said to herself, wishing she'd finished the task before she'd left.

Balto padded into the bedroom and sat down in his dog bed in the corner, watching her sort through the pile of clothes.

"Shall I take this one, Balto? Do you think Jake would like it?" She held up a pretty floral halter dress. Roz had told her the weather would be warm in the daytime, but she'd probably need a sweater or jacket for the evening.

Balto chewed loudly on his toy rabbit, while DeeDee made a pile out of tops, sweaters, a pair of shorts, some pants, and several dresses that she wanted to take to Whistler. When she wasn't sure about an item, she added it to the pile anyway.

"I guess I better take some clothes for walking around the village and boots in case we take a hike in the mountains. I'll also need some sandals for daytime and heels for evening." It occurred to her that she hadn't even started packing her cosmetics and beauty accessories. DeeDee sighed, walked over to the closet, and hauled out her largest suitcase.

CHAPTER TWO

Derek Adams stomped into his small office at the back of the golf pro shop and slammed the door behind him. He stood for several moments trying to compose himself, his heart racing. His chin was jutting out and his face was twisted in a grimace. In other circumstances, he looked a lot more attractive. Cropped, light brown hair framed his handsome thirty-two-year-old tanned face, and with his height and athletic build it was no surprise that he was popular with the ladies at the golf club. While women were impressed with his good looks, the fact that he was a scratch golfer was more impressive to the men who played with him.

"Son of a gun," he blurted out in anger, unable to stop himself from raising his clenched fist and jabbing a golf bag standing in the corner with a right hook. The bag wobbled, and he gave it one more powerful punch for a knockout, sending it tumbling out into the center of the room.

"Ouch," he said through gritted teeth, shaking his sore hand and stretching his fingers in and out several times. *If I wasn't at work right now at the Island View Golf Club, it would be Johnny Roberts sprawled at my feet. Nothing would give me more pleasure than to break a couple of my fingers on that man's smug face. A few smashed teeth would mess up Johnny's good looks, and it might keep him out of the clubhouse for a while.* But as the club's resident professional, unless Derek wanted to lose his job, he knew Johnny Roberts was off-limits. Johnny was a wealthy member of the club with friends on the Board of Directors, and Derek was just one of the hired help. Derek had already crossed the line with Johnny, and might have some explaining to do if Johnny complained to management about the way Derek had spoken to him during an argument they'd just had in the men's locker room.

If I could get my hands on that Rolex watch of Johnny's, I've got several putters I'd like to use to smash it. The thought made him smile, but everyone knew that Johnny never took that watch off. He'd have to think of something else. A firm knock on the door interrupted Derek's next idea, which was throwing a can of red paint on Johnny's big flashy Mercedes Benz.

The door opened and Ron, one of the older and probably the most respected caddie at the club, entered without waiting for Derek's permission. Derek was a more senior member of the golf staff than Ron, but Ron's expression told him it would be unwise to try and pull rank on him at a time like this.

The stony-faced older man closed the door, and folded his arms. If he wondered why a golf bag was lying helter-skelter on the floor in the middle of the room, he made no comment about it.

"Sit down, Derek," Ron said, pointing at a chair. Derek obeyed, while Ron remained standing. His eyes bored into Derek's for several long moments before he continued, "Don't be a fool, Derek. You're young and hot-headed. Johnny Roberts is goading you on and playing you like a violin. He's harmless. Just because he's had a good round or two, it's not a reflection on your golfing abilities. Why are you getting all worked up about it?"

Derek shook his head. He was still angry, but Ron wouldn't understand. "I know I shouldn't have lost my temper in the locker room. Every time Johnny has a good round he acts and talks like he's Arnold Palmer and Jack Nicklaus rolled into one. It's about time the guy grew up."

Ron shook his head. "I think you're mistaken. No one except you seems too worried when Johnny gets a birdie. The members enjoy the game for what it is. It's fun and it's social. I see everything that goes on in this club, and Johnny's a pretty popular guy. So, what's your problem?"

It wasn't just a birdie here and there. The issue was far worse than that. Johnny Roberts was playing better golf than Derek, and today wasn't the first time. Johnny had consistently beat him in every tournament they'd both entered during the last few months. That wasn't how it was supposed to be. The golf pro was supposed to be the best golfer at the club. Derek was sure there was an unwritten law somewhere to that effect. Derek probably could have accepted it if Johnny hadn't constantly bragged about his wins and made the most of rubbing Derek's nose in the score every time he defeated him. It was humiliating, and he was worried the club members might decide it was time to get a younger pro, one that could beat every member in the club, including Johnny.

Johnny had practically said as much during their argument. His words still rang in Derek's mind, "If you don't like getting beat, maybe it's time for you to get a new job, kiddo."

From Derek's perspective, getting fired from a role that was beneath him in the first place was about as bad as it could get. There was a time when he'd been destined for great things in the golf world. Ten years earlier, as a top-ranked amateur player in his senior year of college, he would have been headed for the PGA Tour if it hadn't been for the automobile accident. And now some fifty-year-old man with no hair and a charmed life was showing him up.

"I didn't like his attitude," Derek muttered. "He beat me again today, and I thought he was trying to undermine my position as the club pro. Then he had the nerve to bet he could do it again at our tournament in Whistler."

"So, you called him Noodlehead, which just happens to be similar to the brand name of a well-known golf ball?" Ron chuckled. "That's not very professional at all, Derek. You're acting like a sulky teenager. You better hope he saw the funny side of your remark."

"Yeah," Derek smirked. "I guess." Derek rubbed his neck and tried to get comfortable in the chair. His fit-looking exterior gave away no clues as to his underlying medical problems. The nagging ache in his back was a constant reminder of the terrible traffic accident he'd been involved in, and he had to live with the legacy of that accident every day of his life. The doctors said he was lucky not to have been permanently paralyzed, however, pioneering surgery and several metal pins in his spine had taken care of that. After he spent six months in the hospital followed by a long period of rehabilitation, he still had to exercise daily and have regular physical therapy to keep from being in pain.

On one hand, it was a good thing the accident had happened when it did, since he was a senior near graduation and his golf scholarship had paid for his education. What wasn't so good was that he would never be able to play golf on the pro circuit.

Ron continued, "Maybe you should have thought about it before you made some backhanded innuendos about Johnny fiddling with his handicap. The only thing that accomplished was to make you look like a sore loser."

Derek said nothing, and shook his head.

"Look, I know you've had a tough time recently," Ron said, "but everyone thinks you're doing a great job here. The members admire you and respect you for what you've achieved. What you went through took a lot of guts, just don't blow it, okay?"

Derek nodded. "It took me years to get back to where I am today, Ron. I'm not going to mess it up, I swear."

After many months in recovery, Derek had been able to get a job as a golf pro at a small golf course in Seattle. Over the years, he'd worked as hard on networking as he had on his game, and he'd developed a reputation as a top-notch pro and a great coach. The same tenacity that he showed in recovering from his injuries paid off for the change of direction in his career, enabling him to get his current job as the club pro at the Island View Golf Club. It was a prestigious club, and he enjoyed the status that came with working there.

It was a miracle he could even walk, never mind play golf at the pro level. He had defied everyone who said that he'd never swing a club again. Derek had been the master of his own destiny. He'd thought about the accident a million times over the years, and would forever regret his mistake. He knew at the time he shouldn't have gotten into the car with his roommate who had been drinking beer down at Kite's, the local bar located just off campus in Aggieville. All it took was one stupid mistake, and it had changed his life forever. Now he had to try and fix things the best he could.

Derek stood up and reached out to shake Ron's hand. "Thanks for the pep talk, Ron. I appreciate it."

The firm handshake caused Derek to wince, his hand still smarting from the punch to the golf bag. Ron left the office with a curt nod, leaving Derek alone with his thoughts.

There was no way Derek was going to let this go, despite his conversation with Ron. Derek knew he was a very good golfer, but he wanted to be the best player at the Island View Golf Club, and right now Johnny Roberts was standing in the way of his goal. There was only one way to regain his rightful position, and that was to knock Johnny off the top spot by doing whatever it took to make that happen.

He knew slashing the guy's tires or pouring paint on his car wasn't going to achieve anything. While Ron had been talking to him, Derek had been formulating a more sinister plan. The way he saw it, if Johnny Roberts wasn't around, all of his troubles would go away. Maybe something should happen to Johnny on the Whistler trip. Who knew, maybe it would be his last game of golf, ever. You just never know what the future might hold.

"See ya later, Noodlehead," he muttered as laughed to himself. He turned out the lights and headed for the driving range.

CHAPTER THREE

Jake Rodgers eyed the two suitcases standing in the hallway with suspicion. There was a hard-cased black one on wheels, and a smaller gray leather valise. He scratched his head and looked up at DeeDee, who was holding her breath, waiting for him to say something. Jake's hair was still wet from his morning swim in the Sound. His face softened, and his eyes danced.

"I think there's something you're not telling me, DeeDee. Are you not planning on coming back?" His face broke into a grin.

DeeDee smiled. She was glad Jake wasn't going to make a fuss about her bringing so much luggage for their short trip. It had been a constant bone of contention with her ex-husband, Lyle, that DeeDee seemed to find it impossible to travel light. Jake was far more easy-going than Lyle, and that was one of the many things she liked about him. Although she felt bad about making comparisons between the two men, sometimes she couldn't help it.

DeeDee playfully patted Jake's arm. He wore jeans and a button-down shirt. His handsome face was tanned from the many hours he'd spent that summer swimming in Puget Sound every morning and gardening in the evenings. She'd recently noticed a wetsuit on his porch and wondered if he continued to swim daily all through the winter. There was still a lot about Jake she didn't know, but she was looking forward to finding out.

"I like to travel prepared," DeeDee said, "and so does Balto."

"So I see. Do you have your passport?"

DeeDee nodded and patted her cross-body purse while Balto pawed the floor. He was ready to go.

"Let's hit the road then," Jake said, lifting the black suitcase with ease, not realizing DeeDee had struggled for five minutes to get it downstairs.

DeeDee locked the door while Jake loaded the luggage into the trunk of her SUV. There was also various dog paraphernalia for Balto, including a travel kennel and bed for him to sleep on. Jake's bag went in last, just a small canvas duffel bag. She wondered if it was because of his years serving in the Marines that he was able to keep the contents of his duffel bag down to a bare minimum.

"Is that it? Sure you haven't forgotten anything? Last call for Whistler," Jake said as the final item was crammed inside the car.

Deedee shook her head.

Jake laughed. "Good, because I don't think we could get anything else in the car."

He opened the passenger door for DeeDee before letting Balto jump in the back. It was a short drive to the Bainbridge Island ferry terminal where they would catch the next ferry to Seattle. Balto stood at attention in the back seat, and started to eagerly pant when the SUV stopped at the end of the line of cars waiting for the ferry.

"Yes, Balto," DeeDee said, giving Jake a knowing glance. "We know how much you love the ferry ride, but you have to be a good boy, okay?"

Balto whined, but settled down while they waited for the cars and passengers to disembark from the incoming ferry, before the line they were in started to move. They were traveling after the early morning commuter rush for the thirty-five-minute crossing from Bainbridge Island to Seattle, so it didn't take long to board.

"C'mon, Balto," DeeDee said, when Jake had brought the SUV to a stop on the car deck. DeeDee held Balto's leash while she, Jake, and Balto made their way up the steps to the open passenger deck on the top level of the boat.

It was a cloudy day, and rain was on its way, which was the usual weather pattern for Seattle. DeeDee shivered in her light sweater, regretting that she hadn't brought her windbreaker with her. Jake put his arm around her shoulders, and she huddled into him for warmth as the ferry pulled away from the dock. DeeDee giggled when Balto did his usual trick of trying to nose through the railings to catch the spray from the water below.

"Sit," she ordered, and Balto immediately sat down. Jake gave her an approving smile and kissed the side of her forehead. He'd told her a number of times she was way too soft with Balto.

"I thought we could stop in Vancouver for a walk and then have lunch there," Jake said, above the noise of the ferry's powerful engines. "I'd like to check out Granville Island. Is that okay with you?"

DeeDee's face lit up. "I'd love to," DeeDee said. "I've never been there before. Have you?"

Jake shook his head. "No. We can explore it together."

DeeDee leaned her head on Jake's shoulder as the boat left Bainbridge Island in the distance and Seattle drew closer.

*****

"Shall we play some music?" DeeDee asked, as they settled back in their seats for the drive to Vancouver. She opened the glove box and pulled out a stack of CDs.

"What have you got?" Jake asked, checking the rear-view mirror before pulling into the fast lane of the Interstate, so he could pass a slow-moving truck.

"Um, some of these might be embarrassing," DeeDee said, turning over the cases.

Jake grinned. "I'm not easily embarrassed."

DeeDee gave him an eyeroll. "Okay, let's see. We've got…Garth Brooks, Coldplay, James Taylor and er…" she held a case up and peered closer. "Justin Bieber? That must be one of Tink's. It's sure not mine." She put Justin on the bottom of the stack and continued. "Okay. How about the soundtrack to the Les Miserables movie, or…"?

"Stop right there! Les Mis, please," Jake said, glancing across at DeeDee. She opened the cover and removed the disk. "Good choice," DeeDee said, leaning forward to insert the CD.

"Hey, I forgot to tell you, my singing group is putting on a show," Jake said. "Auditions are next week. I need some practice."

"Hmm," DeeDee said, trying to keep a straight face. Jake's love of singing was not matched by his vocal ability, but she would never want to hurt his feelings. "Well, I guess this is the perfect opportunity. Go for it."

The CD started to play 'Do you Hear the People Sing' and Jake's head immediately started moving in time to the music. He burst into song a few bars in, and DeeDee covered her smile with her hand while Balto whined from his spot in the back seat. Jake sang, and DeeDee hummed as the car sped northwards. They'd left the rain clouds behind them, and the day was brightening. DeeDee felt happy and relaxed. "This reminds me of…"

DeeDee had started to speak, then abruptly clamped her mouth shut. She turned her head away from Jake's startled glance, and looked out the window.

"What?" Jake asked, but DeeDee shook her head.

"Nothing," she said, turning back toward him. "Silly of me. I shouldn't have said anything. Sorry."

Jake frowned, then gave her a reassuring smile. After an awkward pause, he started singing again, and DeeDee reflected on her gaffe. This CD always reminded her of the time years before when she and Lyle had taken a trip to London without their children. They'd seen Les Miserables at the Shaftesbury Theatre, and afterwards they'd eaten at Joe Allen's restaurant in Covent Garden. Robert De Niro was also dining there that night, just a couple of tables away.

She'd wanted to tell Jake that the waitress had said De Niro was charming and had left a very generous tip. Now, thinking it over, DeeDee mentally kicked herself for not sharing the memory with Jake. They'd both spent their lives with other people before the two of them had gotten together, and neither of them was jealous of the other's former spouse. They'd made a decision early on that their past lives were just that – past lives. Watching Jake performing his unique rendition of Les Mis in carpool karaoke, she didn't think he would have been the least bit fazed if she'd told him about the De Niro memory.

They arrived in Vancouver a little after 1:00 p.m., the drive from Seattle on Interstate 5 having taken around three hours. Jake was a fast driver, and even though he'd opted to take the truck crossing at the Canadian border, there had been a delay at Customs. This had given DeeDee and Balto the opportunity to get out and stretch their legs, while Jake and the car snaked along beside them.

By the time they got to Vancouver and Jake found a parking spot, DeeDee was ravenous. At home, by this time of day, she would have already eaten several snacks as well as lunch. Today, apart from some fruit she'd nibbled on during the ride, she hadn't eaten since breakfast.

"I think Balto's hungry," DeeDee said, looking around, "and he's not the only one."

"In that case, let's head straight to Granville Island. Follow me," Jake said, leading the way.

They could have driven to Granville Island, but Jake had said there was a bookstore he wanted to visit, so they were parked in the downtown area. From there they made the walk to the shoreline where they hopped onto the rainbow-colored Aquabus for the ride that took them across the False Creek inlet to the public market and shopping area that was otherwise connected to downtown Vancouver by the Granville Street Bridge.

"It's your lucky day, Balto," DeeDee said to the dog, who showed his pleasure at another boat trip by jumping up and down until DeeDee ordered him to sit.

When they arrived at their destination, there was so much to see on Granville Island that DeeDee wished they could stay longer. She'd heard about how several acres of reclaimed land had been transformed into one of Vancouver's main tourist attractions, and now that she was there, it was easy to see why it was so popular. As well as the Public Market for which Granville Island was renowned, there was a Kid's Market, children's activities and play areas, entertainment including shows and exhibitions, and streets full of shops and restaurants showcasing artisan crafts and food. No mass-manufactured goods were allowed to be sold there. Everything was hand-crafted and original, and many of the artists were available to speak to customers and talk about their work.

"Where would you like to eat?" Jake asked. Every palate and budget was catered to at the Public Market, from casual waterfront cafes to fine restaurant dining to authentic ethnic snacks.

The colors and smells of the food at the Public Market called out to DeeDee as well as pulling at her stomach. She nodded towards the direction she thought they should go.

Jake grinned. "Great, I was hoping you'd want to go that way."

They wandered around the colorful stalls, chatting with the

vendors and sampling different things before they agreed to try the fare at a small Italian restaurant. DeeDee settled on squid ink pasta with soft prawns, tomatoes and chilies, while Jake opted for a porchetta sandwich with sliced figs.

"How's your pork sandwich?" DeeDee asked. It looks delicious."

"It is. Would you like a bite?"

"No thanks, but I'm going to have to remember some of these recipe ideas," DeeDee said. "The tomato and chili sauce from this pasta is just bursting on my tongue with flavor." She offered Jake a forkful to taste, and he nodded in approval. She continued, "I have to provide a sample menu next week for a corporate event I've been hired to cater, and they just want me to serve bowl food. There are some great possibilities on this menu that I could use."

Jake raised an eyebrow and finished chewing. "I've heard that's the new 'in' thing. Personally, I can't see where it's all that much different than serving food on a plate, but what do I know? Anyway, no more work talk on this trip, remember? We both promised. How about if I take Balto for a walk when we're finished here? He can go to the bookstore with me and then we'll meet you back at the car. How does that sound? That way you can putter around for a while without us guys tagging along."

"Thanks, Jake," DeeDee said, squeezing his hand. "I would like to pick up a gift for Roz, so if you're sure you don't want to look around in some of the artisan craft stores, I...." The look on Jake's face told her all she needed to know about Jake and craft stores.

"Very well," DeeDee giggled. "If you insist. I suppose you two better run along. See you in a little while."

CHAPTER FOUR

Wayne Roberts stubbed his cigarette into the overflowing ashtray sitting on the windowsill of his walkup apartment in Seattle. His beefy fingers were stained yellow with nicotine. Wiping his nose with the grubby sleeve of the sweatshirt he'd been wearing for days, he sighed, and headed towards the refrigerator in the cramped small studio apartment. He could walk from one side of the room to the other in three long steps, four if he was feeling lazy, which was most days.

The flickering light inside the ancient refrigerator barely illuminated its meager contents. There was ketchup and milk which were long past their expiration dates in the moldy compartment on the inside of the door, and the glass shelves held some suspect cheese, brown lettuce, and various fast food takeout boxes containing the remnants of Chinese food and pizza.

"Darn it," he hissed, not finding what he was looking for. He ignored the gnawing void in his stomach, because food wasn't what he needed right now. His parched throat and pounding head signaled a greater urgency. There was only one thing that would help him feel better, and that was alcohol.

Wayne's preference was for cheap wine with a twist-off cap. Although as yet he wasn't drinking it from a paper bag in a street doorway, there was a real possibility he might join the ranks of the begging homeless in the very near future. He shook his head in disbelief at how far down his life had sunk, but Wayne wasn't a quitter, no way. He may have fallen on hard times, but it was nothing more than a run of bad luck, or so he told himself. He came from better stock than those losers at his local bar, Fat Al's. Wayne had no time to feel sorry for himself. What he needed was cold, hard cash, and fast.

He grabbed a beat-up leather jacket from the back of the sofa and stuffed his fat arms into the sleeves. As he ran a hand through his greasy hair, the smell of it caused him to pause. He walked over to the kitchen sink, turned the cold water tap on, and splashed his fingers with water. Soap wasn't on his shopping list, and he hadn't enjoyed hot water for weeks. Unpaid utility bills had that effect on a person.

Wayne glanced at his reflection in the cracked mirror above the sink. He barely recognized the red-faced man who stared back at him, and he looked away, choosing instead to remember himself as he had been in better days. Everyone had told him how handsome he was, and although he'd never been short of arm candy in the form of beautiful women, his heart had only belonged to one woman. He was sure his current situation was only temporary. As soon as he got his hands on the money he was entitled to, then he would get Gina back. He was absolutely certain of it.

He stuffed a few loose coins in his jeans pocket, grabbed his cigarettes, and pulled the door closed behind him. At least Fat Al's place would be warm, and he got companionship from the other men who hung out in the bar with him most nights, even if they didn't speak to him much. Once he'd topped off the alcohol in his bloodstream from the small amount that was left from the night before, he knew he'd feel better.

Fat Al's was two blocks away from Wayne's apartment which was located in a rough part of Seattle. The entrance to Fat Al's was an unmarked doorway down an alleyway, but a sequence of six knocks in a precise rhythm gained entry to the dark, smoky den that was open 24/7. Fat Al's was an exclusive club for members of the kind that wouldn't be admitted elsewhere.

Tony, the doorman, greeted Wayne with his usual grunt. Wayne nodded at Tony, and made his way across the dimly lit room to the bar. He smiled at a few regulars, who mostly ignored him. It didn't concern Wayne that the men in Far Al's weren't very friendly towards him, since he knew they weren't his usual type of people. When his money came through, he'd be able to claim his rightful place at any country club he wanted to join, although he wouldn't be going anywhere near the Island View Golf Club, where his older brother Johnny hung out with his cronies. After what had gone down between he and Johnny the previous day, if he never saw Johnny again, it would be too soon.

"What'll it be, Wayne?" asked Fat Al, who was standing behind the bar, drying beer glasses. Fat Al had long frizzy black hair and a matted beard that reached his chest. He was king of the local Harley biker gang that rode out of town in a cloud of smoke on Sunday mornings for their weekly ride.

"Champagne, is it? I'm surprised you came back here after you went to get your money. Thought you'd be off some place swanky, with that woman you're always talking about. Bet she blew you off, didn't she?"

Wayne saw through Fat Al's tough guy persona. It was all a big act for the bar regulars. Rumor had it that on Sundays the bikers stopped for lunch in respectable inns when they left Seattle, and had an annual summer picnic complete with French champagne, plaid blankets, and wicker baskets.

"I'll take the usual, please," Wayne said. "In answer to your question, the money didn't come through yet, but it'll be here any day now, and the woman's name is Gina Cartwright." He dropped some coins onto the bar. *Let Fat Al count them*, he thought.

Fat Al sneered, slammed a glass onto the bar, and filled it with thick red liquid. Wayne reached for the glass and downed it in one long gulp. The initial acrid taste in the back of his throat was replaced by a comforting warm sensation as the wine hit his gullet, and Wayne closed his eyes for a few seconds, letting the enjoyable feeling sweep over him. His entire body relaxed, and he smiled at Fat Al, who was waiting with the bottle in his hand.

Wayne looked at him and said, "Hit me again." After Fat Al had refilled his glass, Wayne lifted the drink in appreciation. He knew he'd have to make this one last.

"So, I'm guessing the meeting with your brother went well?" Fat Al asked, setting the bottle down and wiping the bar with a dirty rag.

Wayne nodded. "Yes, just great." He couldn't look directly at Fat Al and stared down at the bar. "Johnny's going to speak to his lawyer. The letter's being drawn up to release the funds to me." A thought occurred to him, causing him to brighten up. "Hey, how about if I buy everyone a drink to celebrate? Just put it on my tab." A few of the other men in the bar overheard, and raised a cheer.

Fat Al laughed. "I don't think so, Wayne. You just limited out on your line of credit." He looked at the pile of nickels and dimes Wayne had placed on the bar, and pushed them back towards Wayne. He leaned forward and lowered his voice. "Why don't you go home after this one, Wayne? You know you're always welcome here, when you can pay your way."

Wayne was silent while he sipped his drink. He thought back to the conversation with his brother the previous day at Johnny's Mercedes Benz showroom. They were supposed to meet for lunch downtown, but Johnny said he was too busy to leave work due to a golf trip he was hosting in Whistler, British Columbia, beginning Saturday. That meant Wayne had to ride a bus across town to get to Johnny's dealership.

The meeting had not started well. "You're late, Wayne," Johnny had said, looking at his shiny Rolex watch. "I told you I've got a lot to do before heading to Whistler this weekend. What's so important it can't wait until next week?" The older brother laughed mockingly and said, "As if I can't guess."

Wayne had held his tongue, refusing to let Johnny bait him. He saw Johnny's employees watching the meeting through the glass walls of Johnny's office in the corner of the showroom. That attractive woman who wore the low-cut top seemed to take a special interest in the brothers' conversation. Wayne suspected she had a thing for Johnny. He'd wondered if something was going on between Johnny and her, and if Johnny's wife, Cassie, knew about it.

"I'm here to ask you for access to some of the money in my trust fund," Wayne said evenly, choosing his words with care. "As trustee, I need your approval to advance me some of the funds for an investment opportunity. A three-year advance should cover it, since I expect a fast return on my investment."

Wayne had watched his brother's reaction and held his breath, waiting for a response from Johnny. It wasn't the first time he'd been in the position of asking Johnny to release part of his trust fund early. When their parents had died, their estate had been left to the two brothers in equal shares, but Johnny had gotten all of his money up front, while Wayne's was held in a restricted trust fund with Johnny acting as the trustee. Wayne was entitled to a regular allowance for living expenses, but a withdrawal from the fund had to be formally approved by Johnny.

In Wayne's opinion, it was just another example of the favoritism Johnny had enjoyed from their parents at Wayne's expense. Even as children, Johnny had always received better presents. Johnny received a brand-new car from his parents on his sixteenth birthday. When Wayne's sixteenth birthday arrived four years later, he'd been expecting the same. Instead, he got Johnny's old car while Johnny was given a new convertible roadster, practically paid for with the money he'd saved from his part-time job helping a local realtor show properties every hour he wasn't in school.

That was how Johnny had honed his schmoozy sales techniques before he'd skipped college and gone into the high-end car business. While Wayne waited for Johnny's response, Johnny checked his nails and rubbed them on his shirt.

"An investment? That sounds interesting. What did you have in mind, Wayne?" Johnny had asked. "Another one of your get-rich-quick schemes, I suppose. Is it like the alligator burger food truck, or the exercise machines that didn't work?" Johnny had roared with laughter, which drew more attention from the employees and customers in the dealership showroom. Wayne's normally red face had grown even redder.

"Oh no, wait," Johnny had said, slapping his hand on his leg. "I forgot about renting toys to kids. That was the best one yet. Renting to kids with no money who stole the toys or broke them. Well, I gotta love someone who never gives up, Wayne, I'll grant you that. So, what is it this time?"

Wayne had kept his cool, even though he was boiling with rage inside. *How dare Johnny try to make him feel like a fool. It wasn't his fault none of those ideas had worked out, and Johnny knew it. He'd been conned by unscrupulous business partners through no fault of his own.*

Wayne's voice had been shaky, although he'd tried to keep it steady. "It's a racehorse, a thoroughbred, from a great line. This horse definitely has Triple Crown potential. I've been offered one leg, a quarter share. It just needs to win one big race, then we can retire on the stud fees."

Johnny's eyes had widened. "Sounds like a great idea, Wayne. Can anyone else get in? Let me get my checkbook." Johnny had rocked back and forth in his thick, black leather chair with laughter.

On the other side of the desk, Wayne's sweaty hands had clenched the underside of his chair. It had been all he could do not to take a swing at his brother.

"Wayne," Johnny had said, when he'd finally stopped laughing. "do you have any idea why royalty and sheikhs own so many racehorses?"

Wayne shook his head.

"They own them because they're the only ones that can afford to. Do you know much it costs to keep a racehorse? You'll be broke before that horse ever sees a starting gate."

"But..."

Johnny had held up his hand. "What if the horse gets injured, Wayne? What if it breaks its leg?" Johnny had joined his hands together and his knuckles made a sharp crack. "Your investment is gone, just like that."

Wayne had sneered and said, "That's what insurance is for, Johnny."

"Right, and the premiums are so high they're prohibitive. The answer is no, Wayne, and believe me, that answer is final. One day you'll thank me. And may I suggest if you're still thinking about taking Gina to the races, you clean yourself up, get a job, and buy a ticket at the track like everyone else," Johnny had said as he stood up. "Now if you will excuse me, I have a lot to do before my trip this weekend. Your allowance will be in your account at the end of the month, as usual." Johnny had lifted his cell phone and swiped the screen to make a call, while at the same time waving Wayne out of his office.

Wayne's dreams had just gone up in smoke with a flick of Johnny's hand. He was sure his rich brother hadn't given the matter another thought after his departure, whereas Wayne had thought of nothing else. Now, sitting in Fat Al's remembering the scene, Wayne's anger returned. Emboldened by the wine he'd consumed, he remembered a television show he'd seen. He was sure Gina would loan him the money for the bus trip to Whistler when he told her how rich he was going to become. He smiled at the thought.

The only thing standing between Wayne Roberts and his money was that high and mighty brother of his. Wayne knew there was a clause in their parents' trust that if anything ever happened to Johnny, Wayne was to be given his share of the estate outright.

He finished his wine and picked up the coins from the bar. What choice did he have? He'd tried to work with Johnny, but to no avail.

CHAPTER FIVE

DeeDee and Jake took the famous Sea to Sky Highway coastal route on the last leg of their journey from Vancouver to Whistler. It was a spectacular drive along a steep cliff with the road overlooking Howe Sound for a large part of the way, the scenic ocean vista flanked by the mountains in the distance.

DeeDee was glad she wasn't driving, because although she knew it was quite safe, the steep drop-off at the side of the road made her feel dizzy at times. Jake was a careful driver, and since there was very little traffic on the highway, she did her best to relax and simply enjoy the view.

"You okay?" Jake asked, giving her a worried look.

"I'm fine. Thanks for slowing down," DeeDee said. "I just get nervous with heights. I have no intention of taking the Peak 2 Peak gondola ride when we're in Whistler, even though Roz says it's spectacular. I like to keep my feet safely on the ground."

"Not a problem," Jake said, nodding. "We should be there soon. Do you have the GPS details for Roz's place?"

DeeDee laughed. "Um, no. I was just going to ask for directions. I meant to call her earlier, but I'll do it right now."

DeeDee scrolled down to Roz's name on her cell phone and the call rang out through the speaker in the SUV.

"Hi, Roz. It's me, DeeDee. Be careful what you say, because you're on the car speaker phone," DeeDee said when Roz answered the call. "Don't say anything about Jake, because he can hear you."

"As if I would," Roz laughed. "I was worried when you didn't call me back last night. I'm so glad you're still coming, I wasn't sure if you'd gotten my message."

DeeDee and Jake looked at each other in confusion. "What message was that?" DeeDee asked, making a face.

"I left a message yesterday afternoon on your home answer machine saying that we're having plumbing problems in our home. The bad news is, you won't be able to stay here."

DeeDee groaned while a frown crossed Jake's face as he kept his eyes on the highway ahead.

Roz was still chattering as if she hadn't just told them that their road trip was in vain. "The good news is, we've booked you a room at the Fairmont Chateau Hotel. Does that sound okay?"

DeeDee nervously looked over at Jake, who was still staring straight ahead at the road and didn't offer an opinion on the matter.

"Clark's company gets a corporate rate, so it's a steal," Roz continued. "Have you ever seen that place? It's on all the top Whistler hotel lists. It's in a stunning location, situated between Backcomb and Rainbow mountains. It has luxury rooms with king-size beds, swimming pool, gym, sauna…believe me, it's a lot more comfortable than our place. And they do a far better breakfast, of that I'm certain. Frankly, I think you lucked out."

DeeDee could see the corners of Jake's mouth turn upwards as a slow smile started, and she echoed his sentiments. The change in accommodation was an unexpected surprise, but not a bad one.

"I guess we can suffer through it," DeeDee said, grinning over at him. Roz gave them the directions to the hotel from the highway exit, and ended the call by saying she'd made dinner reservations for the four of them at the Grill Room in the hotel for that evening at seven

"Oh, and I forgot to mention that Clark has made arrangements for Jake and him to play golf tomorrow morning. He's really looking forward to meeting you, Jake."

"Yes, me too, Roz. Golf sounds great, thanks," Jake said.

"Awesome. See you later, guys," Roz said, ending the call.

"She sounds happy," Jake said to DeeDee. "What's Clark like? You haven't told me much about him."

"I think he's nice," DeeDee said, "but I've only met him a few times myself. He's in his early forties, so he's a little older than Roz. He's got a good job, never been married, and is quite charming. I understand the company he's with thinks quite highly of him. He's a transplant to Seattle, having moved there from New York. Roz likes him, and that's the main thing that's important to me." DeeDee turned her head and stared out the window.

"Ah, so would it be fair to say you don't approve of him?" Jake asked.

DeeDee turned to him with a puzzled expression on her face. "I didn't say that."

"You didn't have to," Jake replied. "There's something you don't like about him. I can tell."

DeeDee thought for moment about Jake's remark. "I can't put my finger on it," she finally said, shaking her head. "You see, Roz has had some pretty flaky men in her life. I just hope, for her sake, Clark's not another one, that's all."

"I can have Rob, the investigator who works for me, run a check on him if you like. We can have his full life history by morning. If there are any skeletons in his closet, I can find out for you. All you have to do is say the word."

DeeDee scrutinized Jake's face to see if he was joking. She decided he wasn't.

"No, please don't do that. If Roz ever found out, she would consider it unforgivable. It's not my place to intrude in Roz's relationship. What's between Clark and her is none of my business."

"Roz is your sister, DeeDee. You'd only be doing it because you care. If you have a bad feeling about Clark, then you have to go with your gut and at least look at the facts. Best case scenario, you'll set your mind at rest. Worst case, you might save Roz from a future heartache."

"No," DeeDee said firmly. "I have no reason to believe that Clark doesn't have my sister's best interests in mind. I need to give the guy a chance and make use of this time together as an opportunity to get to know him better."

They drove past a sign indicating that the next turnoff was for Whistler. "Agreed," Jake said, as he changed lanes so he could get off the highway. "I can have a man-to-man talk with him while we're playing golf tomorrow and find out his intentions."

"You'd better not," DeeDee warned Jake, whose wolfish grin let her know he was teasing. Even so, she wished the nagging feeling in her stomach would go away. Ever since they'd left Vancouver, something told her they were headed for trouble. DeeDee decided she must be wrong when another pleasant surprise awaited them at the hotel.

"We have an upgrade for you today, to a Junior Suite," the woman at the registration desk beamed, handing DeeDee the paperwork and card keys.

"Thank you," DeeDee said. She decided she could get used to

being wrong. A bellman took their bags and Balto's kennel up to their suite.

DeeDee gasped in delight when she walked into the suite. There was a sumptuously furnished lounge area leading into the bedroom, which had a balcony with a spectacular mountain view. A fruit basket and a champagne bottle chilling on ice had been placed on the coffee table, welcoming them.

"Ooh, look," DeeDee exclaimed, holding up the bottle to show Jake, who had tipped the bellman and was starting to set up Balto's kennel. "There's a card, saying it's a gift from Roz and Clark. We can sample this later."

DeeDee moved the champagne into the minibar refrigerator and then went into the bathroom to freshen up. When she returned, Jake was standing on the balcony, looking up at Blackcomb Peak.

He turned as DeeDee walked out onto the balcony, and pulled her to him for an embrace. "I could get used to this," he murmured, running his fingers through her silky hair.

"So could I," DeeDee laughed. "Shall we explore the village before dinner?"

"Sure," Jake said, lightly kissing her on the cheek. "Give me five minutes, and I'll meet you downstairs."

DeeDee took a warm sweater from the top of her open suitcase and rode the elevator down to the lobby. There were Welcome signs displayed for various groups that were staying in the hotel, and she noticed one for a group from the Island View Golf Club in Seattle. Her ex-husband Lyle was a member there, and DeeDee's stomach lurched at the thought of bumping into Lyle somewhere in the hotel. She would definitely have to warn Jake that was a possibility, although he'd probably see the funny side of the whole thing if it did happen. Running into Lyle was the last thing in the world she wanted to do.

DeeDee and Jake took the shuttle bus from the hotel for the short ride into Whistler village. The village was quiet since the ski season hadn't started yet, but Roz had told her that the build-up for the expected influx of tourists was in full swing. As they walked past sports shops displaying ski clothing and equipment, DeeDee noticed how much the clothing fashions had changed since the one and only time she'd been skiing, years earlier.

That had been one of her and Lyle's less successful family vacations. While Lyle, a seasoned skier, had tackled the steepest runs at Val d'Isere, France, DeeDee and the children were left to their own devices at the ski school. Mitch and Tink, still small at the time, had put her to shame. After a couple of days, they were both proficiently skiing with no poles, with their skis pointed together at the toes, and their heels out wide in the 'Big Pizza' shape shouted out to them by their instructor.

DeeDee hated the chairlift, because she was worried she might fall out. She lived in fear of skiing off the end of the lift in case she was unable to stop, so she decided to retire from the slopes while she still had all her bones intact. She spent the remainder of the week having saunas and massages and indulging in her penchant for chocolate cake.

She and Jake had stopped for a cup of coffee, choosing to sit on a café patio that had outdoor heaters. "I wonder if that's the new ski lift Clark is working on," Jake said as he pointed to the work being done on one of the nearby slopes. The outline of a crane was still visible in the fading light.

"It must be," DeeDee said, looking in that direction. "It looks like it's still got a long way to go to get to the top of that mountain, though. Surely it will take longer than six months to complete it." That was the time frame Clark's company had told him he would be in Whistler when they'd sent him there. He and Roz had been living in Whistler since July, almost two months already.

"I'd say so," Jake agreed. "Maybe they're phasing the construction project. It's probably not possible to make much progress when there's a lot of snow. I'm going to ask Clark how that works. I'll bet it's interesting."

"Yes," DeeDee smiled. She loved Jake's inquiring nature and how he had a thirst for knowledge about such a wide variety of topics.

"Shall we head back and get ready for dinner? I see the shuttle coming." She waved frantically for the little bus to stop, as they ran across the pavement to hop on.

Back at the hotel, Jake offered to take Balto for a walk in the gardens of the hotel, while DeeDee got ready for dinner. She bathed, and unpacked her suitcase, congratulating herself at having the foresight to be prepared by packing a variety of outfits. She selected a black dress and heels and wore her hair up in a loose knot. A statement necklace made from chunky, colorful stones of irregular sizes, completed the look.

Jake, returning from his walk with Balto, let out a low whistle at her transformation. "Wow. You look beautiful," he said, admiringly. "I'm a lucky guy."

A flush rose on DeeDee's cheeks. *I'm pretty lucky myself,* she thought.

While Jake went into the bathroom to shower and change, DeeDee walked into to the lounge area and removed the bottle of champagne from the minibar refrigerator. A selection of crystal glasses was provided on top of the minibar cabinet, and DeeDee set two fluted champagne glasses on the table. A few minutes later Jake came out of the bathroom, looking handsome in an open-necked shirt and casual pants. She poured the sparkling bubbly into the glasses, and with a smile on her face, handed him one.

"To Whistler," Jake said, clinking his glass against hers, and taking a sip.

"To Whistler," DeeDee whispered. In spite of the pleasant moment and the beautiful surroundings of Whistler, she was still unable to shake the uneasy feeling that, for some unforeseen reason, this was going to be a trip to remember.

CHAPTER SIX

"It's over, Greg. I'm sorry, but I'm not leaving Johnny."

Greg Baker listened in disbelief as Cassie Roberts, the love of his life, was ending their fledgling relationship over the telephone.

"Meet me, Cassie. Just to talk, I promise. I know you have feelings for me, and I love you. I swear I'll make you the happiest woman alive if you reconsider your decision." The young man leaned his head on his hand. The day before, he'd asked Cassie to leave her husband Johnny, and he was sure she'd say yes. He had their future all planned out, so her change of heart today came as a shock to him.

"It's just not possible. I'm sorry, Greg."

"What's happened, Cassie? Why not? I know you're not happy with him. You've told me about how he's always at work and never there to help you with the children or spend any quality time with you. You're just his unpaid lackey. Please, you can come and live with me, you and the kids. My house isn't as big as your place, but we'll get by." His voice cracked. "If we're together, I know we can make this work."

He heard Cassie's sigh on the other end of the line. Or was she crying? He wanted nothing more than to be there with her, to comfort her. Greg was sure that if he could just look into her eyes, she'd reconsider and agree to come live with him.

"I can't meet you, Greg," Cassie whispered. "I promised Johnny I'd give him another chance. He knows about us. The babysitter mentioned I'd been out the afternoon we met, and he confronted me. I told him everything."

"Actually, that's good," Greg said. "We don't need to lie anymore. He's a successful, ambitious man. He'll easily find a replacement for you. Maybe he'll learn from his mistakes, and be a better husband to the next woman in his life."

"I don't think you're listening to me," Cassie said softly. "He's promised to be a better husband to me. He's not a bad man, and he loves me. I'm sure of that, plus he is the father of my children. I owe it to him, to all of them, to give him another chance."

Greg thought how typical that was of Cassie She was too soft. She'd let that man walk all over her for years. Johnny Roberts was never home, working around the clock at his car dealership. He was a diamond-in-the-rough type of salesman, not a professional like Greg. Greg might not have as much money as Johnny now, but in the future, when he had his own accounting practice, he could live on Mercer Island if he chose to. But he knew Cassie wasn't interested in material things. She was a down-to-earth homemaker, and her family was her highest priority. For that reason, Greg grudgingly understood Cassie's loyalty to Johnny. She'd never been physically unfaithful to Johnny with Greg, but there was an undeniable attraction between them.

"I just need to know one thing," Greg asked her, "and then I promise never to bother you again. Do you love Johnny?"

She was silent for a few moments, while Greg held his breath.

"Yes, I do. Goodbye, Greg, I wish you all the best."

The line clicked before Greg had a chance to shout, beg, cry, or whatever it would take to keep his dream of a life with Cassie alive.

Today, twenty years later, Greg remembered that conversation word for word, as though it had happened yesterday. He looked at the papers on his office desk. There was the registration form for the upcoming golf trip to Whistler, and a letter from Johnny Roberts inviting the members of the club to join him on what promised to be an unforgettable trip.

Although Greg and Johnny were members of the same golf club, the two men had not spoken in all the time since the episode with Cassie. Johnny had been a gentleman, and never confronted Greg about it. Greg suspected it was because of Cassie's influence, not wanting to cause Greg any more distress. Greg had gone ahead with his own life, and married the next woman he'd dated after Cassie, but it hadn't worked out. Two more wives and five children later, Greg was done. His children were ungrateful brats who didn't care for him, and the feeling was mutual. Greg had established his own accounting practice in the end, but alimony and child support payments for the leeches had sucked him dry. He'd never been able to get the big house on Mercer Island, and now he probably never would.

The door of his office opened, and a pretty young intern entered. Greg remembered hiring her for aesthetic reasons rather than the qualifications on her resume.

"Will that be all, Mr. Baker? I was just about to go home for the evening."

Greg stroked his goatee beard and his eyes traced the young woman's curves. His dark hair was greying at the temples, but he still considered himself attractive.

"That will be all, thank you, Kelly," Greg said. "Are you doing anything special this evening?"

The young woman corrected him. "It's Kerri." She gave him a tight smile that didn't reach her eyes. "And no, my salary doesn't stretch to going out much."

"Maybe we can fix that," Greg said smoothly, his eyes, filled with desire, traveling the length of her body. "If you'd like to have dinner with me later, we could discuss what terms would make you happy."

Kerri's eyes widened and her face flashed bright red. "You should be ashamed of yourself, Mr. Baker," she hissed at him. "You're old enough to be my father."

Greg watched Kerri leave. *So what if she doesn't come back. Interns are a dime a dozen, and they never last long. Next time, I'll hire a real looker who appreciates what I have to offer.*

The problem was, he'd never met anyone else like Cassie. He'd seen her from afar at various events over the years, looking even more beautiful with age. She was always graceful and dignified, and the shorter hairstyle she'd recently adopted showcased her exquisite elfin features. Greg had always thought Cassie looked like a miniature porcelain doll. Each time he saw her, which wasn't often, he wanted to wrap her up and protect her from harm.

They'd never spoken again since that fateful telephone call of long ago, but he'd seen her glance at him when she thought he wasn't looking. From all appearances, she seemed to enjoy a happy life with Johnny, but Greg wasn't so sure. Maybe Cassie had just gotten used to the good life. J.R. Mercedes was an enormously successful business that afforded the Roberts' a luxury lifestyle.

Not only did they have the big house on Mercer Island, there was also a fleet of cars that was updated every time a new model was released. He knew Cassie and Johnny traveled to foreign countries several times a year, and from what he'd heard, there was also a Sun Seeker yacht that Johnny kept moored in Barcelona which they used as their European base. Cassie would be a fool to give up a life style like that.

Maybe she doesn't have to, Greg thought to himself, as a plan started to form in his head. Cassie would be a rich widow if Johnny died. And if something were to happen to Johnny in Whistler while he was at the golf tournament, it would probably just be one of those random sudden death incidents that sometimes occurred to healthy people when they were engaged in playing some type of sport.

Greg lifted his pen and started to fill out the golf tournament registration form. He knew what he needed to do. It was time he sorted things out with Johnny Roberts for good. He could call Johnny and tell him he'd decided it was time to clear the air between them and bury the hatchet. He was pretty sure Johnny would agree to meet him for a cup of coffee. A man like Johnny must have wanted to know what really went down with Greg and Cassie when they were younger.

Oh, Greg would love to bury the hatchet, all right. Right in the back of Johnny's head.

CHAPTER SEVEN

Roz and Clark were waiting for DeeDee and Jake at the entrance to the Grill Room restaurant. DeeDee hurried over to her sister and held out her arms for a big hug.

"Whistler agrees with you," DeeDee said to Roz, first pulling her in close and then standing back. "Let me take a look at you. You're absolutely radiant. It must be the mountain air."

In the two months since her sister had moved to British Columbia, Roz had gained a pound or two, but it suited her, and she had a glow about her that hadn't been present when she'd lived in Seattle. She wore her auburn hair loose, and through the light layer of makeup, DeeDee detected a few new freckles on her cheeks.

"Thanks," Roz beamed. "I've turned into a Whistler person, and with every second business in the village being a cafe, restaurant, or bar, I'm thoroughly enjoying supporting the local economy."

Meanwhile Jake held out his hand to Clark and said, "Hi, I'm Jake Rodgers, pleased to meet you."

Clark met Jake's broad smile with one of his own. "Clark Blackstock. It's great to have you both here. We're looking forward to showing you around." He turned to DeeDee and said, "Roz has really missed you."

DeeDee laughed and took a step toward Clark, who leaned in to kiss her cheek.

"I have not," Roz said as they followed the hostess into the dining room. "Well…maybe just a little."

They were shown to a table in front of the large fireplace that dominated the center of the back wall. The ambience in the room was one of casual sophistication, and a low hum of conversation was audible from the tables that were already occupied. Wood-paneled walls surrounded them, containing areas of glassed-in shelving which displayed the restaurant's selection of fine wine.

The overhead lighting was dim, and a multitude of flickering candles highlighted the polished cutlery, white tablecloths, and napkins. Chairs upholstered in light tan completed the understated elegance of the decor. After they were seated with DeeDee sitting beside Clark, and with Jake and Roz opposite their respective partners, the waitress handed them menus and told them about the specials of the day.

When the waitress had left them for a few minutes so they could look over the menu and wine list, DeeDee reached for her purse and removed a small notebook and pen which she placed next to her table setting.

"I knew it," Jake groaned. "Roz, you need to tell your sister to cut back on her work. She should be spending more time with me, instead."

"Yeah, I thought you moved to Bainbridge Island for a quieter life," Roz said, reaching across the table for the bread basket. She offered it to the others before breaking open a crusty roll for herself. "Instead, you're turning into a workaholic."

DeeDee corrected her. "I moved to Bainbridge Island for a better quality of life, and I hit the jackpot. I definitely found it."

Jake was watching her with an intensity that gave her goosebumps, and she caught his eye, holding his gaze for a moment. She hoped that the look that passed between them conveyed her warm feelings towards him. "I was always planning on working. I just never expected to enjoy my new business so much, or for it to take on a life of its own. I want to nurture Deelish catering to the point where I'm operating at an average of eighty percent of full capacity. If I can do that, I'll have a very good income, and I'll have the flexibility to either ramp up or pull back at any point without getting too stressed or worried about money."

Roz swallowed the bread she'd been eating. "Ooh, listen to you, Ms. Entrepreneur. I think it's marvelous. We should drink to that." She cleared her throat, and pointedly stared at Clark, who looked back at her with a blank look on his face. DeeDee and Jake watched in amusement. "Hint, hint, is somebody ordering the wine soon?"

Clark gestured to the waitress. While he was looking at the wine list, DeeDee took several moments to observe Clark. He was squinting intently at the wine list through horn-rimmed glasses that kept sliding down the bridge of his nose. Tall and tanned, with preppy clothing, the only thing out of place on Clark was a small strand of blond hair that looked as if it had been combed down with the rest, but had broken free. The whole package screamed Ivy League. After a brief consultation with the waitress about wine storage temperature, he ordered a bottle of white and a bottle of red, before pushing his glasses back up the bridge of his nose with his forefinger.

"Are you ready to order your food as well?" the waitress inquired. They exchanged glances and nodded.

"Yes, I think so," DeeDee said, taking the lead. "Is the seafood platter a good appetizer for sharing, or should we order some extra dishes?"

The waitress confirmed that the platter of king prawns, mussels, crab, lobster, and assorted soft fish was big enough for all of them to share.

"Great, and I'd like the rib eye steak for the main course, with a pear salad and a sweet potato and fontina gratin. Thank you." DeeDee smiled at the waitress and handed her the menu. Roz and Jake both opted for steak as well, with Clark breaking rank and asking if he could order something off the menu. After consulting with the chef in the kitchen, the waitress returned and confirmed he could have plain grilled salmon.

The waitress told them the gratin was also large enough for sharing, and Clark ordered an extra side of wild rice with his salmon. DeeDee scribbled some notes about several of the menu items in her notebook as possible ideas for future catering events. She also used the opportunity to note Clark's meal choice in case she ever cooked for him in future. He clearly had a conservative palette.

"I'd like to also order the chocolate tiramisu cake," DeeDee said. She saw the shocked faces of the others and smiled sweetly up at the waitress. "Please bring some extra forks and plates. I'd be willing to bet that they won't be able to resist it when I start eating."

As the wine was being served, DeeDee finished writing and put her notebook away. Clark sampled the red wine, and nodded his approval for the waitress to pour it. Roz took a sip and winked at Clark. "You have great taste in wine. Just like your taste in women."

"Don't I know it," Clark replied, and Roz giggled.

"How do the two of you like Whistler?" Jake asked.

Roz was getting ready to answer when the waitress returned with a server who put a small plate of olives in front of each of them.

"Compliments of the chef," their waitress said. "He's prepared warm olives as the amuse bouche of the evening." She and the server turned and left their table.

When she was gone, Jake turned to DeeDee and said, "What is an amuse bouche? I've never heard that term."

"It's often done in higher end restaurants. The chef prepares something different each evening which is gratis and served at the very beginning of the meal. In French, it literally means what it sounds like, 'to amuse the mouth.' It's just a tiny bite to get your mouth ready for the meal that will follow. Often, it's just one bite of something, but since olives are pretty small, we've each been given three."

"Well, I guess I'm going to learn all kinds of things from you," Jake said grinning.

Roz began to speak. "In answer to your question, Clark's at work most of the time, so I seldom see him. I'm networking, mostly. You know I don't like to overwork myself." Roz was a tax preparer, and apart from a few late filers, most of her work was carried out during the tax season leading up to April 15th. She spent the rest of the year complaining to anyone who would listen about how hard she had to work during the first four months of the year. "I'm hanging out with the chalet maids, ski-bums, and bus boys, all of whom are great fun, but I do wish I had Clarkie to party with."

Clark piped up. "In my defense, it's the nature of the business, especially at this altitude," he explained. "Because of the weather, we need to get to a certain point in the ski lift construction before the first snowfall of the season. The work won't grind to a halt, but once winter's here, there's not a lot we can do. Then, my darling," he patted Roz's hand, "you will get to see a lot more of me."

DeeDee noticed how warmly Clark spoke to Roz, and it was obvious her sister adored the man. Clark's quiet demeanor was yin to Roz's yang.

"When do you expect your work on the ski lift to be finished?" DeeDee asked.

Clark swirled his white wine around in the glass. "It's a three-year project, but the site team changes in rotation. Not many people want to move to Whistler for that length of time, due to their family's needs. There is a possibility we could stay here longer, but that depends on Roz," Clark explained. "I've been asked to extend my contract, but I wouldn't want to stay on here without her."

"Aw," Roz said as she took a sip of her wine, "you're embarrassing me. Time to talk about the golf, I think."

The appetizer was served and the conversation among the four of them was interrupted while they wrestled with shellfish and finger bowls. DeeDee demonstrated how to extract all the flesh from the lobster claws, so that none of it was wasted. Being a seafood lover, Jake was already proficient at the task.

"You're right, Roz. We do need to talk about golf. Are you okay with playing in the morning, Jake?" Clark asked between mouthfuls. "There's a golf outing here in Whistler with some members of the club I belong to back in Seattle. It's the Island View Golf Club. There are about twenty of its members here for a golf tournament. They'll play a round each day, Saturday through Monday, on different local golf courses. I'd like to meet up with the men, but I can only take tomorrow off work, since we're pretty much working seven days a week. The Saturday round is at the Fairmont golf course, which is right down the road from this hotel."

"Will anyone be playing who isn't a member of the Island View club?" Jake asked innocently. DeeDee had mentioned the potential Lyle issue to him on their way down to dinner. As she expected, Jake had shrugged it off. He continued to discuss the arrangements for the golf game with Clark.

"I have no idea," Clark said, "but when I made our reservations I asked if I might bring a guest and was told that it wouldn't be a problem."

"Tomorrow morning sounds good to me. I definitely would like to play, but I didn't bring any clubs with me. Of course, even if I'd known to bring them there wouldn't have been room in the car." He pointedly looked at DeeDee, who smiled sweetly in response.

"No problem, rental clubs are available at the pro shop. Our tee time is 9:00 a.m., and the course is only two or three minutes from here. How about if I pick you up at 8:00 a.m.? That should give us plenty of time to register and hit a bucket of balls on the practice range."

"Perfect," Jake said, as the waitress cleared away the appetizer plates. "And what have you two ladies got planned for tomorrow?"

DeeDee looked at Roz. "Whatever it is, I'd guess that a lot of coffee and sweets of some kind will be involved. At least they better be. Am I right?"

Her sister grinned. "You bet. Clark and I can come here in the morning and the men can go play golf. We can take your car and you can see the house we're renting. After the grand tour, we can go for a walk, stop for coffee and a little bite of something, catch up…"

DeeDee finished her sentence for her. "…then lunch, shopping, more coffee and sweets and possibly wine?"

Roz shrugged. "If you insist, sister dearest."

"I can't wait."

The main courses were served, and the succulent rib eye steaks, or in Clark's case, salmon, were washed down with plenty of wine and laughter. After dinner, Roz and Clark left with a promise to be back bright and early in the morning.

Before turning in for the night, DeeDee and Jake took a moonlight stroll around the hotel grounds with Balto. Arm in arm, they both agreed that their trip had gotten off to a wonderful start.

CHAPTER EIGHT

"Your sales figures for September are up from last month, Mimi. Looks like you're back on target. Congratulations. It's going to be close as to who gets Salesperson of the Year and the large cash bonus that goes with it, but you're definitely in the running. Is there anything else you'd like to discuss?"

Mimi Edmonds viewed her boss, Johnny Roberts, from where she sat across from him at the round table in his glass-walled office in the corner of the J.R. Mercedes dealership in Seattle. Her back was parallel with the glass, because all of Johnny's staff knew he liked to be able to see what was going on in the dealership when he wasn't personally on the floor. Mimi was attending her weekly meeting with Johnny, where they reviewed sales results and targets, as well as discussing any other issues concerning her work.

She was one of his best employees, so it was usually a short meeting. Today, however, she lingered, seemingly reluctant to leave. "As a matter of fact, there is," Mimi said, sucking in her cheeks which had the effect of emphasizing her plump lips. She leaned forward, her sole intention being to present Johnny with a clear view of her ample cleavage. Ever since she'd started working at the dealership two years ago, she'd had a thing for Johnny Roberts, but so far, he'd ignored the various attempts she'd made to flirt with him. Mimi knew that slow and steady won the race, or so the old saying went, but she felt that tactic was getting ridiculous and certainly not producing any results. No man had ever resisted her charms before, and Johnny Roberts wasn't going to be the first.

When she'd turned forty a few months earlier, Mimi knew that the phrase 'Forty and Fabulous' didn't really do her justice. In addition to her career goals, she had high personal standards that she maintained at all times. *Perfect and poised* was her motto. She'd progressed from a 'plain Jane' type of California girl to an immaculately groomed Seattle sophisticate. The highlights that sun-kissed her shoulder-skimming already golden locks were hand-painted on by the stylist with the longest waiting list in the city. It took sweat, tears, and patience to get on that list. She treated her manicurist, facialist, nutritionist, personal stylist, and personal trainer like family, in fact, they'd taken the place of the suburban working-class parents and sister she'd left behind in San Diego and was always too busy to visit. The sparkling crystal rocks gleaming on her ear lobes, fingers, and wrists were the real thing, because in Mimi's case, diamonds were her best friend. Mimi had always gotten what she wanted, and she wanted Johnny.

"I think we both know that there's something...unsaid between us," Mimi murmured, reaching her right hand up to her already revealing sheer blush-colored silk blouse and unbuttoning it a notch lower. Her breasts nearly spilled over the top of her delicate lacy bra.

Johnny remained impassive and maintained eye contact with his employee, rather than looking at what Mimi was obviously displaying.

Mimi held her position, deciding that the best option was the direct approach. Johnny was a no-nonsense kind of guy, and she figured he'd probably appreciate that type of approach.

"Do you find me attractive, Johnny? Because the feeling is mutual," she said in a husky voice. Mimi watched Johnny watching her, and imagined what it would feel like when he kissed her. They would have to be discreet, of course, but she'd been in similar situations before. The fact that Johnny had a ring on his finger didn't bother her.

"You're a very attractive woman, Mimi," Johnny said "and I'm flattered by the implied offer, but I'm a married man."

Mimi smiled, revealing her perfectly even teeth. Her dental veneers had been fitted shortly after she arrived in Seattle, sixteen years earlier. Her own teeth were uneven and unsightly, and adult braces revolted her.

She didn't skip a beat. "I'm not interviewing for a husband, Johnny, just a lover. Call it a business deal. We're both good at those."

Johnny stretched back in his chair, looking relaxed. "I appreciate your honesty. Have you ever been married, Mimi?"

Mimi was surprised Johnny had asked. Most people assumed that Mimi had never been married, because that was the impression she liked to give. Her backstory was of a survivor, an average girl without a college education who had made good. When she recounted her journey from Michelle Edmonds, working the cash register in a food market in her hometown, to Mimi, pulling down a six figure a year income and driving a top of the line Mercedes SLK, she always omitted the part about Ken and Josh. Something made her decide to open up to Johnny. Better that she was honest with him, if they were going to have a relationship. Then he would understand why his marriage wouldn't be threatened by her.

"Yes. Married at eighteen, widowed at nineteen." She shrugged, keeping her composure, deciding at the last minute not to reveal that she had a son. "Ever since then, I've had a no strings attached policy with men. My heart will always belong to someone else, the man who was my husband and died tragically at such a young age. Believe me, your wife has nothing to worry about."

"Since you know what it's like to love someone, Mimi, that's how I feel about my wife. I almost messed it up once, and I won't take that chance again. I've had other offers before you, and the answer's always the same. Why go out for a hamburger when you can have steak at home?" Johnny guffawed, pleased with his joke.

Mimi glared at him. He was starting to annoy her now. This was not the way this conversation was supposed to go at all. She tried a change of direction. "You cheated on your wife before? So, what happened? Did she give you another chance, and you're afraid to blow it?"

"No, it was…" Johnny shook his head. "Never mind, it's ancient history. What I have with my wife, Cassie, is solid. We almost split up because of something that doesn't even matter anymore, but in the end, it brought us closer together. We both realized we had too much to lose."

Mimi's face hardened, and she laughed bitterly. "You're a sentimental fool, Johnny. You only live once, as my dead husband could tell you. We can have a little fun together, and no one will ever know."

"No, Mimi, I'll know. I'm not prepared to jeopardize my marriage for you or any other woman. It's not a reflection on you, believe me. That's just how I roll."

Mimi folded her arms, jutting her chest out. "I see. In that case, I'll need to consider how this may change our working relationship. I can easily get a position somewhere else where my talents are more appreciated, like Northern BMW, for instance."

Johnny chuckled. "Mimi, of that I have no doubt. As far as I'm concerned, we can forget that this whole conversation ever happened." He tapped the side of his nose. "L.A Confidential. J.R. Mercedes would be sorry to lose you, but that's a decision you'll have to make. Why don't you think things over, and let me know what you've decided when I get back from Whistler next week?"

A wave of disbelief washed over Mimi, but there was no way she would let Johnny see how mortified she felt. She gave Johnny a quick nod, and thought she saw pity in his eyes. *Have some dignity,* she said to herself, standing up and willing her body to stop trembling. She'd learned all about dignity after Ken had died, and she'd held her head high and walked tall ever since. Stares from co-workers and customers followed her as she left Johnny's office, fumbling to close the top button of her blouse.

Back in her own office it was another story. *How dare he*, she fumed, sitting at her desk in the small office she shared with Nick, who managed the corporate leasing side of the business. She was glad Nick was out of the office on a lunch break, because he would have asked her what was wrong, and she might not be responsible for what she might say right now. Every time she rewound the conversation with Johnny in her head, the playback got worse. Not only had Johnny rejected her, he'd compared her to a hamburger. And then he'd had the audacity to laugh! That was the worst insult anyone had ever directed at Mimi, and there had been a few.

And as for Cassie Roberts, what a joke she was. Mimi had seen her when she stopped by the dealership occasionally to see Johnny. She was a pathetic, tiny little woman with a convict hairstyle, whose signature look favored comfort over style. *How could he want to go to bed with her instead of a hottie like me?* Cassie also had an annoying habit of talking to the employees and asking about their families. She knew everyone's name, and Mimi thought that was just creepy as well as being intrusive. Cassie had a boring job at a museum, did charity work, and probably had hairy legs.

Mimi poured herself a cup of coffee from the machine in the corner of the office. She picked up Nick's newspaper and sat down at her desk. If she could just take her mind off the whole episode, she could decide what her next move should be. The fact that Johnny would be away for a few days later in the week gave her some breathing space.

Glancing at the whiteboard on the wall, she could see the rows of pins stuck in it, with each one representing a sale of hers and indicating how close she was to hitting her monthly and annual sales quotas. The incentive bonus plan at J.R. Mercedes was structured in such a way that she would lose all of her lucrative accrued bonuses if she quit any time soon. Walking away from J.R. Mercedes and leaving that kind of money on the table was not a viable option for Mimi.

She leafed through the newspaper, skimming over the usual sensationalist headlines, while a part of her mind began to form a plan that would allow her to avenge the slight she'd just gotten from Johnny. The solution was very simple.

Mimi called her son, Josh, who had moved to Seattle after he'd recently finished his prison sentence. Every time she thought of the scar he'd gotten from one of the inmates when they'd had a fight, it sickened her. He'd been the spitting image of Ken before the scar, but now his handsome face was a distant memory, and the resemblance to Ken was only in her mind.

"Good morning, Josh. I have a little something I'd like you to take care of for me." She listened to him for a minute and then said, "Josh, if you take care of this, I'll be happy to continue to give you a monthly allowance, and I think it's time I even raised it. Here's what I'd like you to do," she said, explaining what she had in mind. When she'd ended the call, she sat back in her chair, satisfied with the plan she'd made.

If Mimi couldn't have Johnny, Cassie shouldn't have him either. Let Cassie find out what it's like losing a husband, Mimi thought. She'd survive, just like Mimi had, but Cassie had the luxury of a large inheritance to soften the blow. For Mimi, there was even a bonus involved in her plan. She wouldn't have to live with the shame of having to work with Johnny after the way he'd turned her down and utterly humiliated her.

She heard Johnny laugh from the showroom.

Stupid man. He just messed with the wrong hamburger.

CHAPTER NINE

Jake was waiting outside the hotel when Clark and Roz drove up to the entrance promptly at 8:00 a.m. Jake could see Roz gesturing animatedly to a bemused looking Clark, who raised his hand to greet Jake.

Roz jumped out of Clark's jeep, leaving the door open for Jake. "Hi Jake," Roz said, "Where's DeeDee?"

"Upstairs, feeding Balto," Jake said. He told Roz the room number and explained to her that the elevator for suites was located to the left of the lobby area.

"DeeDee and I can take her car," Roz said. She nodded toward Clark, who was waiting inside the jeep with the engine idling. "You jump in with Clark to go to the golf course. See you later back at Chalet Whistler de Roz, otherwise known as Clark's and my place."

"Okay." Jake watched Roz as she quickly walked into the hotel to meet DeeDee. Jake knew that DeeDee was excited about spending the day with her baby sister. Over breakfast, they'd discussed Jake's impression of Clark, which was positive.

"Women read too much into everything," was all Jake had said about the matter. "You always think there has to be some inside story on everything. Clark doesn't strike me as having anything to hide, and I consider myself a pretty good judge of character. So, he's either a man of few words, or he can't get a word in edgewise what with all of Roz's jabbering."

Jake had to quickly lean to one side to avoid DeeDee's aim at him with the breakfast menu card. He tsked, "Too slow. I'm a trained Marine, remember? Special Ops. You can't get a menu over on me."

DeeDee had laughed. "You do have a point about Roz," she'd said, spreading manuka honey on her wholegrain toast. "Clark must be some kind of a saint to put up with her constant talking."

Jake turned and walked towards the waiting jeep with a smile, and got in beside Clark who drove the short distance to the golf course. Jake waited while Clark removed his golf clubs from the back of the jeep, and then the two men walked towards the clubhouse.

"Some of the members from the Island View golf trip are over there," Clark said, as they approached the group of about half a dozen men standing at the registration table. The men were a mixture of ages, and Jake wondered if any of them was Lyle, DeeDee's ex.

"Jake, this is Greg Baker," Clark said, introducing him to a man with a nicely trimmed goatee beard.

"Jake Rodgers," Jake said, extending his hand to Greg, who responded with a nod and a handshake that had all the personality of limp lettuce.

While they registered for the tournament, Clark continued talking to Greg. "We're going to get Jake some rental clubs and then hit a few shots on the practice driving range."

"It's a shotgun start at 9:00," Greg said, "so everyone begins at the same time, but from different tees. Check which tee you're on, and make sure you give yourself enough time to get there by 9:00."

Jake looked at his watch. "In that case, we better get moving," he said to Clark. "I've developed a bit of a slice that needs some work before we start."

A bucket of balls later, Jake and Clark had bonded over a mutual love of golf and a competitive spirit that had Jake looking forward to seeing which one of them would triumph with the lowest score for the day. Just as Jake had suspected, Clark was perfectly capable of holding a conversation without Roz present. The mood between the men was relaxed as they loaded their clubs into a golf cart, and Jake drove toward their designated tee box which Greg had informed them was the nearby first tee.

Several of the other Island View Golf Club members were driving away, one by one, each heading in a different direction as the players made their way to their respective starting points.

Clark raised his hand to shade his eyes from the sun as he and Jake approached the first tee box. He looked towards something laying on the grass, then he squinted and pointed to a heap on the ground. "What do you suppose that is? Looks like someone has fallen."

Jake swerved the cart to where Clark had pointed. As they drove closer, they realized the person laying on the ground wasn't moving. The cart had barely come to a stop when Jake leaped out. Striding across the grass, he took in the situation in an instant. The body wasn't just motionless, it was lifeless. He held up his arm to warn Clark, who was a couple of steps behind him.

"It looks like Johnny Roberts," Clark said from where he stood.

Jake moved closer to the body. "You know him?"

Clark nodded. "Yes, he's part of our group. He's the one who organized the trip for the Island View members to come to Whistler."

As Jake processed this information, something about the name sounded familiar to him. He crouched down and reached his right hand under the side of Johnny's chin, pressing two fingers gently on his neck to feel for his pulse, but there was none. There was no sign of trauma to the body, and it was still warm. Jake immediately swung into action, moving Johnny into the recovery position on his back before attempting CPR.

"Call 911," Jake ordered Clark in between mouth-to-mouth resuscitation attempts and forcefully pumping his hands up and down on Johnny's chest. By the time the sirens could be heard in the distance, Jake had conceded defeat.

He stood up and shook his head at Clark, whose face had a stricken look on it. "He's gone. I can't get him back." Jake did, however, remember where he'd heard the name before.

"Is Johnny's wife's name Cassie, Cassie Roberts?" he asked Clark. "Do they live in a big house on Mercer Island?"

Clark replied in the affirmative. "Yes, that's them."

Jake rubbed his chin. DeeDee's neighbors at her home before she moved to Bainbridge Island had been a family named Roberts, and DeeDee and Cassie were friends. He explained the situation to Clark.

"I know you and the other members of the club can identify Johnny, but I think it might be comforting for Cassie if DeeDee makes the formal identification of the body. They're very good friends, and Cassie would probably feel better knowing that it was DeeDee. This is going to be a huge shock for her, and DeeDee too, come to think of it."

Jake looked grim. "Would you please call Roz and ask her to break the news to DeeDee and also see if Roz can drive her here in DeeDee's car?"

Clark nodded, and tapped the screen of his cell phone.

Jake turned to face the commotion behind them. The arrival of Emergency Medical Services at the clubhouse had drawn the attention of other golfers on the course. As the paramedics approached the spot were Johnny was laying, so did several men from the Island View golf group.

"Thanks, Clark. I'll see if I can contain this until DeeDee and Roz get here."

*****

A short time later, Jake stood with his arm around a red-eyed and tearful DeeDee, who nodded her head. "Yes," she said. "That's Johnny Roberts."

She could hardly believe that Johnny, the big friendly giant of a man she'd lived next door to for over twenty years on Mercer Island, was laying dead on a gurney in front of her. She hadn't seen Johnny since she'd moved to Bainbridge Island, but there he was, as tanned and handsome as ever, with his distinguished white mustache, shiny bald head, and chunky Rolex watch. She'd know him anywhere. He even looked like he was smiling. DeeDee had never heard Johnny raise his voice or say a cross word to anyone.

"He looks like he's sleeping, doesn't he? Peaceful," DeeDee said. She was emotionally overwhelmed and feeling vulnerable, as she looked up at Jake for guidance. She allowed herself to be wrapped up in his arms.

"You're in shock, DeeDee," he said, steering her over to Roz, who had a worried look on her face. Jake went back to stand with Clark and several other men who knew Clark.

"I can't believe it," DeeDee whispered. "I feel so bad for Cassie."

Thirty minutes earlier, DeeDee and Roz had been giggling like teenagers about their respective relationships and swapping stories about people they both knew, oblivious to the drama that was unfolding on the golf course.

"Poor Cassie. Wherever she is right now, she has no idea that her life is about to be changed forever, and she'll never again see Johnny alive. Her children will never see their father alive either." DeeDee started crying again, and Roz attempted to comfort her by gently patting her on the back.

DeeDee whispered in Roz's ear. "Can you check something for me please?" She watched and waited while her sister went over and pulled Clark aside from the other men, then made a phone call before returning.

When Roz came back she glared at DeeDee. "I can't believe you made me do that," she said. "I have confirmed that Lyle is not in Whistler, he is definitely alive, and at work in his office in Seattle. Your children still have a father."

"Thank you," said a sheepish DeeDee.

Jake and Clark were talking to the two Royal Canadian Mounted Police Officers who had arrived on the scene riding their trademark shiny black horses. There was a low, muted conversation among the men prior to Jake and the oldest police officer approaching the sisters.

"Inspector Dudley Stewart, ma'am," said the police officer in a stiff voice, tipping his tan hat to DeeDee. He wore the Royal Canadian Mounted Police uniform, which was a tailored red military gold-buttoned coat with a black belt and epaulettes, black leather gloves, black jodhpurs riding pants with a yellow stripe down the side, and tan riding boots. The holster on his belt contained a pistol. Inspector Stewart looked sternly at DeeDee, who practically jumped to attention.

"I was explaining to Mr. Rodgers that I will be the person in charge of the investigation into the unfortunate death of Mr. Roberts," Inspector Stewart said to DeeDee in a monotone. "There are no signs of foul play, but nothing can be ruled out until the coroner conducts an autopsy."

DeeDee inwardly groaned. This was all starting to feel like familiar territory as she thought back to a murder that had occurred during the first ever dinner she'd catered on Bainbridge Island. *No wonder I had a bad feeling about this weekend,* she thought.

"Mr. Rodgers tells me you are good friends with the decedent's wife and that you will notify her personally?"

"Yes, officer, er...sir," DeeDee mumbled.

"Fine," Inspector Stewart said. He turned to Jake. "Please get in touch with me if Mrs. Roberts thinks of anything that may be relevant to our investigation."

"Of course," Jake said, shaking the Inspector's hand.

DeeDee watched the two police officers ride way with a loud clip clop of hooves, steeling herself for the toughest phone call she was ever going to have to make.

CHAPTER TEN

Roz poured some steaming hot coffee into a cup and pushed it across the table in the lounge of DeeDee's suite at the Fairmont hotel. A pale-faced DeeDee had just emerged from the bedroom. Easing herself into the comfortable chair opposite Roz, she heaved a sigh of relief as she sat down and looked down at the coffee.

"Well?" Roz asked. "How did Cassie take it?"

DeeDee was silent, as she gazed up at her sister. She added two sugar cubes to her coffee, and stirred and stirred. Finally, she found her voice.

"Very upset, as you would expect of anyone who just got the news that their husband had dropped dead. At least she was at her job at the Seattle Art Museum, so other people were there who could provide her with some support. She said she'll call her children and ask them to meet her at her office, so she can tell them in person. The plan is for all three of them to drive here to Whistler. They should all be here in a few hours to claim the body and make arrangements to have it sent back to Mercer Island."

"I don't envy them the trip," Roz said. "The weekend traffic on Interstate 5 will be horrible, but I'm sure they'll want to get here as quickly as possible."

DeeDee nodded, sipping her coffee. The bitter taste of the coffee was at odds with the sickly-sweet aftertaste of the sugar overload, but sugar was a comfort that DeeDee reserved for stressful situations such as this one. "Cassie said her son, Liam, will drive them up here. She said she wouldn't be able to do it, because she's so distraught."

"That seems perfectly understandable," Roz said. "How old are her children?"

DeeDee thought for a moment. "They're close in age to Mitch and Tink. They all played together when they were young children. Liam must be about twenty-four now. He's in medical school. I'm pretty sure Briana is twenty-one. There was a big party for her at Cassie's home on Mercer Island last year. It was one of the last parties Lyle and I went to together before he moved out. Of course, it was a total sham, since by then Lyle was already sleeping with his new lover, but for some reason we both cared what the neighbors thought. When I think about it now, it seems ridiculous, but there you go." She managed a hollow laugh. "I called Mitch and Tink to let them know about Johnny's death. They're both upset, because they thought the world of Johnny. They probably knew him better than I did."

"What was he like?" Roz asked her sister.

DeeDee looked up at Roz. "Johnny was larger than life. He was loud and funny, but if you didn't know him he could come across as obnoxious. Lyle played golf with him quite a bit, and I remember him commenting that Johnny rubbed a few people the wrong way when he was on the golf course. I don't think there was any malice in it, it was just Johnny's idea of fun. He believed in living life to the fullest, that's for sure."

"That sounds like a good approach to life," Roz said thoughtfully. "You never know what's around the corner. I remember meeting Cassie at your home, years ago. As I remember, she's kind of a small, quiet woman, isn't she?"

DeeDee smiled. "Yes, she might come across like that, but

Cassie's quietness is her strength. She's very easy-going, compared to Johnny. I think she had to be, to keep the peace in that house."

"That sounds interesting, what do you mean. Did they fight a lot?"

DeeDee shook her head. "No, not at all. At least, not that I knew about. I never heard shouting coming from their house, if that's what you mean. They had very different parenting styles. Johnny was very strict with the kids when they were growing up, and I think Cassie acted as the mediator to make sure everyone got treated fairly. She seemed to be a lot more lenient than Johnny."

Roz leaned in. "In what way?"

"Well, a good example is their daughter Briana. She's not the academic type at all. Liam aced his way through school and as I said, is studying to be a doctor. It's all he ever wanted to be since he and Mitch used to cut up worms and dissect the dead birds they found in the yard when they were small boys. It turned out that Briana had more of an entrepreneurial bent. She decided she was going to skip college like her father had, but Johnny wouldn't hear of it. He threatened to disinherit her if she didn't go to college and graduate."

"What happened?" Roz asked. "You'd think a self-made man like Johnny would want to support her entrepreneurial spirit."

"Exactly," DeeDee said, patting Balto, who had padded across the suite from his bed to stand beside her chair. "It's kind of surprising, but Johnny was dead set against it. In the end, Cassie had to intervene. They came up with a compromise that gave Briana two years to make it in her chosen career. She could live at home, but she received no financial support from Johnny and Cassie. If, when the two-year time period was up, she wasn't financially independent, she agreed that she'd enroll in the local community college."

Roz's mouth fell open. "Please tell me there was a happy ending."

DeeDee grinned. "There sure was. Briana apprenticed with

Danielle Laruen, the well-known Seattle interior designer, for a year before starting to take on her own clients. She did small jobs that weren't prestigious enough for Danielle. When the two years were up, she moved out of the Roberts' home when she was only twenty, and rented a small studio with an apartment upstairs. Last I heard, she'd just won the contract to provide the interior design for the furnishings in a new five-star hotel on the Seattle waterfront which is being built by an international hotel chain. Johnny told everyone who would listen that he was the proudest father on the planet. He took all the credit of course, while Cassie said nothing, which was typical of her."

Roz shook her head sadly. "Right now, Cassie's going to need all the strength she can muster to get through this ordeal. The fact this happened so far from home is going to make everything even more complicated."

DeeDee's hand flew up to her mouth. "Oh dear, I almost forgot. She asked me if the police will allow the body to be taken out of the country, since the cause of death hasn't been established. I'm not really sure, but Jake might know, or he could find out from Inspector Stewart. There's something else that Cassie said, that's worrying me…" DeeDee stopped talking, then shook her head. "Never mind, I shouldn't have said anything."

Roz's eyes narrowed. "Are you sure? If there's any way we can help her, it might be important."

"No," DeeDee said, "it wasn't anything like that. It's just…she kept repeating over and over that it was all her fault, something about what she'd done to Johnny. I have no idea what she meant, but she said she'd explain everything when she got here. I tried to tell her not to blame herself, and that there was nothing she could have done to prevent his death, but she was adamant."

Roz scratched her head. "Cassie was miles away when Johnny died. Apparently, the police don't think there is anything suspicious about Johnny's death. You don't think…"

"Absolutely not," DeeDee said, her eyes widening. She gave Roz a horrified glance. "I can't imagine Cassie was involved in any way. She said she spoke to Johnny last night, and that they'd had words. She was hoping to clear it up this morning but he hadn't called before he…he… well, you know." DeeDee sniffed.

"Croaked," Roz said with a nod. "She probably just feels guilty that they argued about something the night before he died. What a sad thing to have happen. It winds up being your last memory of someone you loved," Roz said shuddering.

DeeDee was pensive. "It sounded like it was more than just a petty argument, but I hope I'm wrong. I guess we need to wait until she gets here to find out." She glanced at her wrist watch. "What time did the men say they'd be back? It's way past lunchtime, and I'd better take Balto for a walk before he jumps off the balcony and makes a run for the nearest tree by himself."

The women watched Balto, who had moved to the door and was impatiently waiting with his leash in his mouth.

"They didn't," Roz replied, "but I'll call Clark and find out. Why don't you go out with Balto, and we can eat here in the room when you get back? I'll order room service while you're gone."

"Thanks, Roz. I would prefer to eat here rather than go downstairs to the restaurant," DeeDee said, standing up, and patting the side of her thigh to call Balto over. She gave Roz a grateful smile, as she hooked Balto's leash to his collar. "I'm sorry this has ruined our plans for today, but I think I should stay close to the hotel and wait for Cassie to get here. She asked me to make reservations for her and the two children. I hope you understand."

"Of course," Roz said. "I'll stay and have lunch with you. If there's anything at all that Clark and I can do, just let us know."

"Okay," DeeDee said, opening the door. She was halfway out, with Balto pulling on the leash in front of her, when she turned back to Roz. "Oh, and by the way…what was that thing you were going to tell me earlier, just before Clark called with the news about Johnny?"

"Oh, it was nothing," Roz said, waving her sister on. "I can't remember anymore. Go on with Balto. What? Why are you giving me that funny look?"

DeeDee's gaze lingered on a blushing Roz for a few more seconds before she finally followed her sister's directive.

"Hmm, Balto," DeeDee said on their way down the hallway. "Roz is a terrible liar, don't you think?"

CHAPTER ELEVEN

The topic of conversation among the men at the golf club was all about Johnny, and what could have possibly happened to him at the first tee box to cause his untimely death. Jake and Clark stood at the edge of the group, waiting for an announcement about the golf tournament.

"I'd be very surprised if it goes ahead as scheduled," Jake said in a low tone.

"I agree," Clark said, looking around the reception area, "but I'm just wondering who's in charge of the Island View group now that Johnny's not around. Looks like Ron, one of the caddies, is talking to the Fairmont pro. I think he was helping Johnny organize things. Maybe he knows something." He nodded toward a gray-haired man wearing a yellow sweater and navy pants who was huddled in conversation with a couple of the Fairmont Golf Club officials, recognizable by their club blazers.

One of the men standing beside Jake and Clark turned around. "We were just saying that Johnny would be in his element if he was here. He loved nothing better than taking charge in a crisis." The man chuckled. "He's still the center of attention even when he's dead. He's probably looking down right now, thinking how no one will ever forget the Whistler golf tournament. Well, at least he died happy, doing one of the things he loved best. Maybe if the golf hadn't gotten him, the marathon would have."

"He was training for a marathon?" Jake asked. "That's pretty impressive at his age."

A couple of the other men standing nearby joined in the conversation. "He'd already reached his target of raising twenty grand for charity for the New York marathon he was going to run this November," said one. "I'll bet he just overdid it. A man his age training like a twenty-year old? His ticker probably got him in the end."

"No," said another, shaking his head. "I disagree. Johnny told me his doctor had given him a clean bill of health before he started training for the marathon. He took his fitness training very seriously. Johnny told me one time that he knew his limits, but he felt the marathon was a once in a lifetime opportunity, and he wanted to experience it."

"He was fifty something, wasn't he?" Clark asked. "Did he smoke or drink?"

"He was fifty-two," said the second man. "He had an occasional drink, but he wasn't a smoker. Johnny took all the right precautions with his health. You can say what you like about Johnny, but he wasn't stupid. He ate very healthily, and he worked out daily. That guy popped nutritional supplements like candy. For the past six months, he'd been running several times a week with a marathon trainer. He said he trusted the experts to make sure he peaked at the right time, then he was planning on easing off. It's a shame he didn't make it to the marathon. I liked Johnny, and I'm really going to miss him." The man lowered his head, and there was a murmur of assent from the others present.

Jake, who'd been listening to the conversation about Johnny with interest, spoke up. "So, you don't think it's likely that Johnny died from natural causes?"

The men looked at each other, and several of them shook their heads, indicating no.

"My girlfriend is good friends with Johnny's wife, Cassie," Jake explained. "I'm a private investigator, so if anyone can think of anything that might help put her mind at ease about what happened to Johnny, please let me know. I've explained to the local police officers that I'll pass on any information that might be relevant."

Their conversation was interrupted by an announcement from the Fairmont golf pro saying that Saturday's golf tournament was canceled out of respect for Johnny.

The official went on to say, "Snacks and lunch will be provided for everyone, and I've been asked to advise you that there will be an open bar, courtesy of the Fairmont Hotel."

"Johnny would have wanted that," Ron piped up, his voice cracking.

"Hear, hear," said a voice from the back of the crowd, and a few people laughed. The men dispersed, either making their way to the locker room or to the restaurant and bar areas.

Jake was waiting for Clark, who had gone to speak to Ron, when he felt a tap on his shoulder. He turned to face a sandy-haired man with pale skin and freckles.

"I'm Ray Wentworth," the man said to Jake, shaking his hand. "I couldn't help overhearing what you said just now, about you being a private investigator. Do you have a minute for me to run something past you?"

"Yes, sure thing," Jake said, waiting for Ray to continue. Jake noticed Ray looking over his shoulder to see if anyone else was listening. "How can I help you, Ray?"

"It might be nothing, or it might be important. The thing is, if you're wondering about whether foul play could be involved in Johnny's death, and I think you are," he said, looking pointedly at

Jake, "then there's something you should know. There was a recent incident at the Island View Golf Club between Johnny and the golf pro there, a man by the name of Derek Adams."

Ray spoke so quietly that Jake had to lean in to hear what he was saying. He could smell coffee on the man's breath.

"Go on," Jake said, stuffing his hands in his pockets. "What happened?"

"It was Johnny being, well, Johnny, I suppose. He wasn't the most modest of men," Ray said, by way of explanation. "Johnny had beaten Derek in a golf competition. Derek, being the pro, can beat everyone else at the club, but Johnny's been the exception these last few months. Johnny's been on a bit of a roll, and he was rubbing Derek's nose in it. Derek wasn't too happy about it, to put it mildly."

Jake's eyes narrowed. "How did Derek react?"

Ray's eyes widened. "He was angry, and he lost his temper. Said some things he shouldn't have."

"Like what?"

"Well, for starters he suggested that if Johnny was playing so well recently, wasn't it strange his handicap hadn't been lowered. He asked him who had been marking his score card." Ray looked at Jake. "Johnny wasn't a cheater, everyone knows that."

"From what I've been hearing, Johnny was quite a character," Jake said. "It sounds like he knew how to press people's hot buttons."

"Yes, that's precisely what he did," Ray said. "Derek was already mad, and Johnny bet him a hundred bucks he could beat him here at Whistler. He said if Derek was such a hot shot pro, how did he explain that an old man like Johnny could beat him so easily? Then Derek said that Johnny was trying to get him fired from the club. Johnny responded by saying Derek was doing a good enough job of that all by himself, so he obviously didn't need Johnny's help. Derek started shouting that Johnny would be sorry he'd ever said that. Ron, the caddy you see over there, had to intervene to split them up. I thought Derek was going to punch Johnny, and then he really would have gotten himself fired."

"I'll certainly investigate this further. Thanks Ray," Jake said. "Is Derek on the trip this weekend?"

"He should be around here somewhere, although come to think of it, I haven't seen him."

"Okay, I'll see what I can find out," Jake said shaking Ray's hand again. "I appreciate it, Ray." Ray gave Jake a nod and headed off.

*****

A short time later, when Jake and Clark returned to the hotel, DeeDee greeted Jake with a long hug. She held him tight, not wanting to break the clinch. It had been an emotional day, and she'd missed his quiet strength.

"I'm so happy to see you," she whispered, resting her head on his chest. "Roz and I ate before one of the employees who's a friend of hers took her home. I hope you're not hungry."

"Hush," Jake said, rubbing her back before maneuvering her toward one of the club chairs in the lounge area of their suite. He gently pushed her into the seat and then sat opposite her, in the chair Roz had sat in earlier. The room service tray was still on the table, and most of the food Roz had ordered was still on it. Although she'd been hungry, when the food arrived DeeDee found she didn't have the stomach for more than a couple of bites.

"I had a sandwich at the golf club," Jake said, running a hand through his cropped salt and pepper hair. "I was talking to some of the men about Johnny, trying to find out if anyone knew anything that might be relevant concerning his death." Jake sighed. DeeDee poured two glasses of water from the decanter on the table, and handed one of them to him.

"Thanks," Jake said, before downing the water in several long swallows. DeeDee poured him another.

"Did you learn anything useful?" DeeDee asked, sipping her water.

"Possibly," Jake replied. "The general consensus is that Johnny was healthy, and if he died from natural causes it would be quite a surprise. There's always the possibility he had a heart attack, but I have a feeling there's something more sinister going on. One of the club members pulled me aside and told me Johnny had an altercation with the Island View golf pro who apparently has a grudge against him. Seems like there might be at least one person who could have had a motive to do him in."

Jake smiled somberly at DeeDee and said, "And where there's one, in my experience, I'm sorry to say, there's usually more. Were you able to talk to Cassie?"

DeeDee recounted her conversation with Cassie. When she got to the part about Cassie saying it was all her fault, Jake rubbed his chin. "That's a strange thing for her to say. Do you have any idea what she might have meant? Do you think Johnny and Cassie were on good terms, or was there some sort of trouble brewing between them?"

DeeDee shrugged. "That's what Roz was asking, too. There's nothing that I know of, but I've hardly seen Cassie since I moved to Bainbridge Island. I never suspected marriage trouble between those two in all the time I've known them, but after Lyle and I split, Cassie said she never saw it coming either. I didn't really share it with anyone, apart from Roz."

"We can find out the details from Cassie when she arrives. What time did she say she'd be here?"

"As soon as possible," DeeDee said. "I've made reservations for the three of them to stay here at the hotel tonight. There's something else I'd like to discuss with you, Jake, but you're probably not going to like it."

"How so?" Jake asked, his eyes twinkling. "I don't think there's anything you could say that I wouldn't like, DeeDee, but I'm a big boy, so shoot."

"It's just that Cassie will probably want the body sent back to Mercer Island as soon as possible. I'm sure she'll be returning to Mercer Island right away. I expect there will be a big funeral. I'd like to leave Whistler tomorrow to go back with her, and see if there's anything I can do to help. After what's happened, I wouldn't be able to enjoy the rest of our time here." She looked over at Jake, judging his reaction. "Cassie will really need someone there to help her, whether she knows it or not. Even if it's only making tea for guests or tidying up her home. Her children are going to be dealing with their own grief, and I don't think they'll be much help, plus they really shouldn't have to do it."

Jake reached across the table and squeezed DeeDee's hand. "I think that's a great idea. You're a good friend, DeeDee."

DeeDee gave Jake a half-smile. "We can come to Whistler another time, when this is behind us. I think we're overdue for some quality time together."

Jake looked at DeeDee. "It's a deal, but on one condition."

"Name it," DeeDee said.

"I want to go with you. I'm between cases at the moment, and Cassie might need the help of a private investigator. At least it's sure starting to look that way."

DeeDee felt the warmth of Jake's hand, still holding hers. *This man is definitely a keeper*, she thought as she smiled at him.

CHAPTER TWELVE

DeeDee and Jake were waiting in the lobby of the Fairmont Chateau Hotel when Cassie and her two children arrived that evening. The smartly dressed, middle-aged woman and her children looked like all the other guests arriving for a weekend stay in Whistler, except they had no luggage.

"We came straight from the museum," Cassie explained in her ever-present calm manner. As usual, she was dressed in a classic and unassuming outfit. She wore a simple string of pearls, a crew-neck pale blue cashmere sweater, and a matching pencil skirt with low-heeled shoes. Her children towered above her, both taking after their father in the height department. There was not a hair out of place on Cassie's cropped pixie hairstyle, but DeeDee could tell from the pain in her friend's hazel eyes that inside her heart was breaking.

"Jake, it's wonderful to finally meet you," Cassie chattered, after DeeDee had introduced him. "I've heard from DeeDee that you're the man who has been making her so happy." She beamed at DeeDee, her eyes brimming with tears, before turning back to Jake. "Jake, this is my son Liam, and my daughter Briana."

The two young adults were also composed, shaking Jake's hand and kissing DeeDee. Liam looked just like Johnny, DeeDee thought, with his prominent jawline and handsome face. Liam's unruly mop of black hair showed no signs of thinning, despite the fact that Johnny said his own baldness had started when he was in his twenties. Although Johnny was known for exaggerating things, DeeDee suspected that may have been one case where he was telling the truth, since Johnny had been bald the whole time she'd known him. She hoped Liam would be able to hold on to his raven locks for a few years longer than his father had.

"I'm so sorry about Johnny," DeeDee started, her chin trembling. "I…"

"Oh, DeeDee," Cassie said, shaking her head and raising a finger to her lips. "We have to stay strong. There's so much that must be done. Liam and I are going to the morgue." She looked at her son, who nodded. "Would it be alright if Briana stays here with you? She doesn't feel strong enough to see her father right now." Cassie gave Briana an encouraging smile, but Briana wouldn't meet Cassie's eyes and stared at the floor.

Cassie continued talking, "We can check into our rooms when we return, or Briana can do it for us while we're gone. Hopefully, we'll only be here for the one night."

"Absolutely," DeeDee said, exchanging a worried look with Jake. "Cassie, do you want Jake to go to the morgue with you? I'm not sure if I told you that he's a private investigator. He's already spoken to Inspector Stewart about getting Johnny's body released, so if there are any issues that come up he might be able to help."

"Thanks, Jake," Liam said, speaking up on his mother's behalf, "but I think we're good. Mom spoke to the coroner already. The release form will be signed once the autopsy has been completed. We can't set a date for the burial until the coroner releases the body to the local funeral home here in Whistler. Once the funeral home takes custody of the body, they'll transport it back to Mercer Island." Liam put his arm around Cassie, and DeeDee thought Cassie looked even smaller than usual, despite her heels.

"If you and DeeDee could look after Briana, we'd appreciate it," Liam said. Briana's head tilted upwards, and she looked at Jake through the long messy strands of dark hair which obscured her face.

Liam glanced at his sister and looked back at DeeDee and Jake. No further words were necessary to explain his concern. Anyone could see that Briana was in no condition to go anywhere. Through her long dark hair, the young woman's sunken eyes were rimmed with red, and her pale cheeks were streaked with makeup and tears. DeeDee wanted to scoop her up and tell her everything would be okay, except that was a promise she couldn't make.

"Of course. We'll keep an eye on Briana while you're gone," Jake said as he walked Cassie and Liam towards the main entrance of the hotel. The three of them talked a little longer before Cassie and her son walked out into the fading early evening light.

Meanwhile, DeeDee ushered Briana towards a cluster of chairs in the corner of the lobby. As they crossed the room, DeeDee noticed Briana's step was uncertain and her legs were shaky. "Sit here," she said, patting the girl's shoulder. DeeDee thought what an attractive young woman she'd become. Her alabaster skin contrasted beautifully with the dark color of her hair, and sculpted brows framed the piercing blue eyes that sat above razor-sharp cheekbones. Although tonight, from what DeeDee could see, those eyes looked vacant. Briana sat down heavily, and DeeDee took a seat beside her.

Jake strode over with a serious look on his face. "I'll take Balto out for a walk," he said, sizing up the situation. "and give you ladies some space." He smiled at Briana and kissed DeeDee on the forehead before walking away.

"He's cute," Briana said, watching Jake from under her hair as he left.

DeeDee leaned across and lifted Briana's hair out of her eyes, tucking it behind her ears. "Look at you," she said, morphing into a mother's role. She wiped Briana's splotchy cheeks with a clean tissue from her purse, leaning back to admire her work. "That's better," she said with a smile. "So you think Jake's cute, huh? I'm glad you approve."

She was pleased that Briana managed a half-smile in return. "Yep, for an old guy. How long have you two been dating?"

"Not long, about six months," DeeDee said. In some ways, it had seemed like longer.

"Do you think my mom will date again? I don't want her to."

Briana looked like a sulky little girl to DeeDee. Her bottom lip curled out the same way DeeDee had noticed it many times before when she, along with DeeDee's daughter Tink, had done something they shouldn't have when they were younger, and they'd been caught.

"Oh, Briana. I'm sure that's the last thing on your mother's mind right now. You'll have to ask her how she feels about that, but I don't think she'll be rushing into anything."

Briana stared at DeeDee. Her manicured hands were clasped together tightly on her lap, and DeeDee noticed they were trembling. "Can I tell you something?"

"Of course," DeeDee said. Briana's face was expressionless, and DeeDee waited for her to speak.

"I think my father was having an affair." Her voice was a flat monotone. "He denied it, of course, but now I'm not so sure. I don't know what to think. We argued when I found out about it. He said it was nothing, that the woman was stalking him, and that Mom didn't know. He made me promise not to say anything." Briana paused and twisted her fingers in her lap. "Whatever I decide to do, I feel like I'm lying to Mom, or else betraying my dad. But Mom knows something is up, I'm sure of it. She's been acting really weird, even before Dad died. If he was having an affair, I can't tell her now. It would hurt her even more. What do you think I should do?"

DeeDee was speechless. A million thoughts had been flying through her mind all day, but Johnny being unfaithful to his wife hadn't been one of them. Johnny Roberts adored the ground that Cassie walked on. Whatever had been going on between Johnny and

Cassie, and Cassie had promised to tell her later, DeeDee was a strong believer that children should not be involved in their parents' problems. However, it seemed that in this case, Briana had already been dragged into the middle of whatever was going on, and there was no going back from that.

DeeDee had a nagging feeling in the back of her mind that the information may in some way be relevant to Johnny's death. But however much DeeDee sympathized with Briana's wish to protect her mother, she knew in her heart that there was only one answer she could give her.

DeeDee took a deep breath and slowly began to speak, "I'm a big believer in the truth, and that it has its own way of getting told. I also believe that speaking to your mother about this might set your mind at rest. However much you want to shield her from more heartache, it could be a simple misunderstanding or something she knows about already. If it's bothering you, I think you should get it out in the open. I know your mother can deal with it, but you have to let her decide what to do with the information, Briana."

Briana looked unsure. "Okay," she said eventually, "but I need to tell you this as well, in case…anything happens. I'm scared, DeeDee. My dad was acting weird that day. I don't want anything bad to happen to my mom, and if Jake is a private investigator he might be able to help us. Please?"

"Of course," DeeDee said with some reluctance. "Tell me what happened, Briana."

Briana's face lifted, and she began to speak. "It was a couple of weeks ago," she said, leaning in towards DeeDee. "I was downtown at a business meeting, and Dad called me. 'How's my girl?' he asked, you know the way he did…" Briana stared into the distance before focusing back on DeeDee. "Anyway, we met at a nearby Starbucks. We used to do that quite often to catch up on things. Sometimes Mom would join us." She smiled, and her face lit up, remembering Johnny. "On that particular day we were talking, just me and Dad, and then someone phoned him…"

Briana bit her lip. "It was a quick conversation. I couldn't hear what the caller was saying, but I could tell whatever the person said made Dad upset. He cut the conversation short and told the person never to phone him outside work unless it was an emergency. He also told the person that he couldn't meet with them to discuss the issue, because he was busy with his daughter. When he ended the call, he acted really strange." She shook her head, and twisted a strand of her hair around her finger.

"I asked him what was going on, and he refused to discuss it in any detail. He just said there was a woman at work called Mimi Edmonds who had told him she liked him, if you know what I mean, but it was nothing to worry about. When I pressed him about it, and asked if anything had happened between the two of them, he swore it hadn't. Then he admitted she was practically stalking him. He was pretty sure he'd seen her driving by the house, and things like that."

"Well," DeeDee said. "it sounds like you have your answer. Why would your dad lie about it?"

"I don't know, but I asked if Mom knew about it, and that's when he made me promise not to tell her. He said Mimi needed to get professional help, and he'd take care of the problem. I asked why he didn't just fire her, and he said that she was one of his best salespeople, and if she left, J.R. Mercedes would lose a ton of sales. He told me every other dealership in town wanted her to work for them, so he needed to be very careful."

Without knowing the whole story, DeeDee considered that Briana had a point. Something was fishy about the phone call, and she wondered if there was more to it than Johnny had admitted to. "I'm sure your father was dealing with the situation in the best way he knew," she responded. It was the only thing she could think of to say, but if she'd hoped it would reassure Briana, it was ineffective.

Briana shrugged. "DeeDee, you know my dad wasn't afraid of anyone. That's why I thought maybe they were having an affair, and she had something on him. Maybe she's psychotic and wanted to do something to hurt my mom. If so, I think it's better to tell Mom before she does. Something was up with Mom and Dad recently, and I think this woman might have been the problem. That's why I wondered if Jake could find out more before I say anything to Mom."

DeeDee's mind was racing ahead. *Like it or not*, she thought to herself, *you're up to your neck in this, DeeDee Wilson.* Looking on the bright side, she told Briana there was a good chance that Jake might be able to help.

After all, it was possible Mimi Edmonds might be a lot more dangerous than Briana imagined.

CHAPTER THIRTEEN

It was a tired and stressed sounding Cassie who telephoned DeeDee's suite later that night.

"I'm sorry it's so late," Cassie whispered. "I sent Liam to bed to get some sleep, since we have to leave in the morning to go home and make the funeral arrangements. I wonder if you could come to my room for a few minutes, so we can talk?"

DeeDee had made reservations for separate rooms in the hotel for Cassie, Liam, and Briana, to allow each of them their privacy. Briana had checked in right after she'd shared her worries with DeeDee about the situation between her father and the woman at his car dealership.

"I hope you and Jake won't mind if I eat alone in my room," she'd said. "I'm not feeling very sociable right now. Please don't think I'm being rude." DeeDee had assured her not to worry and told her she'd see her in the morning.

Jake and DeeDee had eaten dinner, and Jake had gone out with Balto for one last time, leaving DeeDee surfing through the channels on the hotel television, waiting for Cassie to get back from the morgue and call her.

"Of course," DeeDee said, pulling on a robe. "You're on our

floor, so I'll be there in a minute."

Cassie was also wearing a hotel robe when she opened the door of her room for DeeDee. The thick white toweling fabric dwarfed her tiny frame. "Come in," she said with a limp smile. Inside the room, she pointed to a bottle of white wine on top of the minibar that was already open. "Will you join me in a toast to Johnny?" And then, Cassie crumpled onto the bed, sobbing hysterically.

DeeDee sat on the edge of the bed beside her, with an arm around Cassie's shoulder, sensing the raw grief that had consumed Cassie and permeated the air in the room. A rerun of the television sitcom Friends was on in the background, the canned laughter a stark contrast to Cassie's muffled sobs. The two women didn't speak for several minutes. There was no need for words at that moment, and no words would have been adequate given the circumstances.

Cassie finally stopped sobbing, sniffed, and blew her nose. She looked up at DeeDee. "I could use another glass of wine." It was a statement, not a question, and DeeDee nodded while Cassie poured. The women sat at a table in the corner of the room, the bottle of wine between them.

"It's all my fault," Cassie said in a dull monotone voice, her emotions now under control. She repeated what she'd told DeeDee earlier on the phone. "It's my fault Johnny's dead."

"Cassie…" DeeDee began. "You don't know what happened yet. You can't blame yourself."

"Oh, but I do," Cassie said, as she calmly sipped her wine. "There's something I need to tell you, DeeDee. I don't know if you were aware of it, but Johnny and I had our problems. I suppose all married couples do. You've been through it, so I know you'll understand."

DeeDee's heart sank. She didn't want to believe that Briana had been right about Johnny having an affair. "I'm sorry to hear that, Cassie," DeeDee said. "Was Johnny playing around? Briana…well she mentioned earlier that she was afraid of something like that."

Cassie smiled. "That girl is a such a worrier, but I'm the reason she's been worried about her parents' marriage ever since she was a little girl. You see, I almost had an affair once. Yes, I can tell you're surprised."

DeeDee's mouth had fallen open, and she took a large swallow of wine to cover up her shock.

"It was a long time ago," Cassie explained. "The children were small, and Johnny was working a lot. Actually, we never saw him. I knew he was doing it for us, so I didn't blame him, not really. But…I resented the fact he didn't seem to appreciate it was hard work for me doing everything else, essentially being a one-parent family."

DeeDee nodded. "I understand what you're saying. It's really tough when you're going through it. Who was the other man? Do I know him?"

"I doubt it, although he is a member of the Island View Golf Club, so you could have met him. His name is Greg Baker," Cassie said.

DeeDee raised an eyebrow. "No, I don't know him, but I think I've heard the name. Go on."

"Johnny volunteered for a charity event at the golf club, but Johnny being Johnny, forgot all about it. It was to be a fun outing for underprivileged children. Oh, he showed up on the day the event and acted like a big shot. As a gift for the children he'd arranged for some toy pedal cars to be delivered to the golf club, and the kids got to pedal them around in the parking lot. Each of the toy cars looked like a miniature Mercedes Benz, and they were a big hit with the kids. He presented rides on the pedal cars as gifts.

"However, I was the one who had stepped in to help organize the event. It was a pitch and putt mini-golf tournament, and Greg was in charge of raising sponsorships for each hole from local businesses."

She smiled. "Believe me, he took it very seriously."

"Tell me about him," DeeDee said.

"He was the opposite of Johnny," Cassie said. "Quiet, serious, soft-spoken. He's an accountant, and all we did was talk," she said, her eyes shining. "He was there for me when I needed someone. He listened to me. Everything about Johnny was a whirlwind, and Greg was slow, deliberate, and solid as a rock. I felt like Johnny didn't really care, and that we'd become like two ships passing in the night. For a while it seemed to me that maybe Greg was The One, and I'd settled for Johnny too soon. All the same, I wasn't planning on doing anything about it. I didn't think Greg was either. Boy, was I wrong."

"What do you mean?" DeeDee asked.

"It all came to a head after the charity event was over. I was kind of relieved, since I thought Greg and I needed some space. In the back of my mind I thought we both would come to our senses and everything would blow over. But Greg called me, and begged me to meet him. I told him no, that it would be a mistake, but..." Cassie closed her eyes and swallowed. "We arranged to meet one afternoon. I hired a babysitter to watch Liam and Briana. When we met, Greg professed his undying love for me, and asked me to leave Johnny."

Cassie bowed her head and raised a hand to her forehead. "I felt torn, DeeDee," she said, looking up. "I really did care for Greg, but I realized in my heart that I loved Johnny, and I wasn't about to break my vows to him. I should have told Greg outright, but I took the easy way out. I didn't want to hurt him."

"What was the easy way?"

"I told him I'd think it over. The next thing I knew, it all blew up."

"Oh no," DeeDee exclaimed. "What happened?"

"Johnny confronted me that night and asked me where I'd been that afternoon. He said he'd called our house, and there was no answer. I told him I'd taken the children to the park. My lie fell apart, because he'd actually spoken to the babysitter when he called. He asked me why I was lying. I told him everything."

A single tear trickled down Cassie's cheek. "Johnny and I talked for hours that night. Everything was on the table, our hopes and fears for our relationship, and where it had all gone wrong. At one point Briana asked why mommy was crying. She didn't understand what it was about, but she's never forgotten that night. She asked if daddy was leaving, and we told her no, of course not. We tried to assure her that mommy and daddy were going to be okay. We did our best after that, and we were more than okay."

"I know you were," DeeDee said, reaching out for Cassie's hand. "You and Johnny were a great couple. What happened to Greg?"

Cassie's voice went flat again. "He called me the next day and asked me when the children and I were coming to live with him. I told him I was staying with Johnny." She looked up at DeeDee. "I think he really loved me, DeeDee, and I broke his heart," she said. "For that, I'm truly sorry, and I'll carry that guilt with me forever. We never spoke again, although I've seen him at various golf club functions."

DeeDee looked at the empty wine glasses. "What did Johnny say to Greg?"

"Johnny never said a thing to Greg. They saw each other at the golf club, and it made him uncomfortable, knowing that Greg had tried to have an affair with me. I made him promise he'd never say anything, and he kept his word, knowing it was best to put the whole thing behind us. I know how much I hurt Johnny, and I think that a little part of it always stayed with him, but we managed to move beyond it. But Greg, well I think it's been festering away at him for years." Cassie's hand gripped the edge of the table. "In fact, I'm surprised Greg never killed Johnny."

Cassie's words hung in the air, and a chill went down DeeDee's spine. She shivered, noticing the thin drapes blowing in the breeze from the open balcony door, and pulled her robe tighter. She thought maybe she'd misheard Cassie.

"Cassie, did you just say something about Greg killing Johnny?"

"Yes," Cassie said in a matter-of-fact tone of voice. "Briana was right that there's been tension between Johnny and me lately. It was mostly about work. Johnny has been consumed with some problems there recently. I don't know the details, all I know is that he was stressed and anxious. I've been telling him for months he should sell the business and retire, but he wouldn't hear of it. If it wasn't for Greg Baker, I'd be the first to think Johnny might have keeled over from a heart attack. But..." she shook her head, "not now."

The bottle of wine on the table was still half-full. DeeDee estimated that Cassie couldn't have drunk more than two small glasses, so it wasn't the wine talking.

"The last time I spoke with Johnny was late yesterday," Cassie continued, "and we argued...about Greg. Johnny said that Greg was in Whistler, and he wanted to meet with Johnny this morning for coffee."

"Why?" DeeDee asked. "Why now, after all this time?"

Cassie's mouth was set in a thin straight line. "That was exactly my point when I urged Johnny not to meet with him, but Johnny was a big softie. He said it was time to let bygones be bygones, and if Greg wanted to apologize to him I shouldn't worry my pretty little head about it." Cassie let out a low sigh, and her cold stare sent another chill through DeeDee's bones.

"DeeDee, the way Greg looked at me the last few times I saw him gave me the creeps. I didn't mention it to Johnny, but Greg frightened me. That's why I didn't want Johnny to meet him. And now..."

DeeDee's heart was pounding. *And now Johnny's dead.*

CHAPTER FOURTEEN

Later, while the two women were still sitting at the table in Cassie's room, DeeDee stared at a sheet of hotel notepaper with a name and telephone number written on it in Cassie's neat handwriting.

It had the name of Wayne Roberts on it and a Seattle area code and telephone number.

"Are you sure you don't mind making the call?" Cassie asked DeeDee followed by an audible sigh. "I just, I can't face speaking with him right now." It was Cassie's turn to shiver. "I know it's late, but I really should let him know tonight. After all, he's Johnny's brother, and his only surviving relative since their parents died a number of years ago." Cassie tapped the pen in her hand on the tabletop, pursing her lips.

From the way Cassie spoke of Wayne, DeeDee could tell he wasn't Cassie's favorite person in the world. Although DeeDee vaguely recalled that Johnny had a brother, she'd never met him, nor had she heard either Cassie or Johnny talk much about him. She was sure he hadn't been a regular visitor at the Roberts' home when she lived on Mercer Island, or she would have remembered him.

"No problem," DeeDee said.

"Use the hotel phone," Cassie suggested. "He might not pick up if it's my Caller ID, and believe me, you don't want him to know yours."

"You're really selling this guy to me," DeeDee said with a laugh. "Is there something I should know about him?"

Cassie raised an eyebrow. "You'll find out soon enough."

Holding the piece of notepaper in her hand, DeeDee sat on one of the twin beds. She read the number that Cassie had written and tapped it into the hotel phone that was on the table between the two beds.

The gravelly grunt that answered after it rang a couple of times caused her to move the receiver away from her head. The grunt was followed by a raspy cough that sounded like the person was about to spit a wad of phlegm in her ear. DeeDee made a face at Cassie, who was hovering above her.

"Um, hello. Is this Wayne Roberts?" DeeDee asked, in her best telephone voice.

"Who wantsta know?"

"My name is DeeDee Wilson. I'm a friend of your brother, Johnny, and his wife Cassie."

The sound of a slurp and gurgling reached DeeDee, followed by a loud belch.

"And?"

"I'm afraid I have some bad news," DeeDee said. "Johnny passed away earlier today. Cassie asked me to let you know. She'll be in touch with you about the funeral arrangements when the details have been finalized." She looked up at Cassie, who was nodding.

DeeDee waited for Wayne to say something. It sounded like a match was being struck, and she heard Wayne take a deep breath.

"Well," ain't that somethin'," Wayne said, exhaling with a loud breath into the phone. His voice was quieter than before. "Poor old Johnny. I'm sorry to hear about it. Please tell Cassie I'll be over tomorrow, to pay my respects and all that. Of course, we'll also need to sort out the paperwork for my money."

DeeDee squinted, trying to comprehend what he was saying. Wayne was still talking, waxing lyrical about family, friends, and how death was a great equalizer. He was saying something about it not mattering how rich you were when you were dead, because you couldn't take it with you.

"Now it's my turn, DeeDee," Wayne slurred, "and they'll all see what great good comes to those who wait. Oh yes. My time has definitely come, and anyone who ever crossed me can eat their words and bow at my feet." The tone of his voice changed and he said, "Maybe we could go out for dinner some time, DeeDee, watcha' say?"

"I'm not sure what my boyfriend would think about that," DeeDee answered, grimacing at Cassie. "I understand you're upset right now, Wayne, and I'm very sorry for your loss."

"You're darned right I'm upset," Wayne said, with a loud snort. "Will you tell that woman, Cassie, Johnny's widow, that I expect to get what's coming to me, okay? Johnny's not around to hold the purse strings any more. What's mine is mine, and she can't do anything about it. No more delays. You got it?"

DeeDee was taken aback by Wayne's snarly tone. "I'm not sure what you mean, Wayne," DeeDee said. "Cassie's out of town right now, and she's very busy trying to make the funeral arrangements, but if you could explain what you need, I'd be happy to pass the request on to her."

"She knows," Wayne said. "Don't let her fool you. She's a wolf in lamb's clothing. You know, the Ms. Butter-Would-Melt-In-Your-Mouth type. That's why she's gotten you to do her dirty work. I'll be waiting to talk to her, DeeDee, when she gets home. You tell her, okay? Uncle Wayne ain't goin' nowhere except straight to the bank with his money."

The line clicked, and DeeDee was left speechless.

"Good grief. He's a real charmer," DeeDee said, replacing the receiver like it was something dirty she didn't want to touch. "He didn't sound very upset about Johnny. Actually, I think he may have been drunk."

"It is after 10 p.m. on a Saturday night," Cassie said with a glance at the clock. "Although from what I know of him, I think he's like that most of the time. What did he say, apart from asking you out on a date?"

"Something about getting his money," DeeDee said. "He was sort of rambling, and I really couldn't make any sense out of what he was saying. He said you know all about it, and he wants what's his and you've got it or something like that. He claimed he was upset about Johnny, although he sure didn't sound like it. What on earth was he talking about?"

Cassie sat on the other bed, her knees opposite DeeDee's. "Johnny's parents put money in a trust fund for both of their sons," Cassie began. "Due to various indiscretions over the years, Wayne's trust fund was restricted. Johnny had control over what Wayne could, or rather it was mostly what he couldn't, do with the money. However, the trust conditions specified that if anything happened to Johnny, Wayne would be entitled to his money in full, with no restrictions. I assume that's what Wayne was referring to. When you told him about Johnny, all he could see was…"

"…dollar signs," DeeDee interjected.

"Right," Cassie said. "Not that the money will last him long. I expect he'll blow through it in a year or two, maybe less, depending on how much he owes people. That's what always happened in the past, and it was why Johnny was so strict with him. He knew what Wayne was like."

"In what way?"

Cassie thought for a moment. "Wayne was always a dreamer, gullible, and an easy target for scammers. He went from one guaranteed get rich quick investment to the next, and the outcome was always the same. The investment went bad, or something went wrong that Wayne hadn't thought of. Of course, it was never his fault. He always had an excuse why that particular scheme didn't work out, but he went on living the high life anyway, partying and surrounding himself with women that were real losers, until Johnny pulled the plug. You can guess what happened."

DeeDee looked up at the ceiling, tapping her index finger on her cheekbone. "Um, Wayne wound up on skid row, his so-called friends deserted him, and it was all Johnny's fault?"

"Something like that," Cassie said. "Johnny was trying to protect Wayne from himself, but Wayne never saw it that way. He had a chip on his shoulder when it came to Johnny. It's a shame, since Johnny would have loved nothing more than to mentor Wayne and help him succeed. It never happened, because Wayne is one of those people who every time he buys a lottery ticket, is convinced that this time he's going to win the jackpot. Of course, he never does."

DeeDee noticed Cassie raise a hand to her mouth and stifle a yawn. "You need to get some sleep," she said softly to Cassie.

"I won't be able to sleep, DeeDee, and I really I don't want to." Cassie closed her eyes for a second and shook her head, her eyes jolting wide open again. "Because if I close my eyes I see Johnny, and that reminds me he's not coming back." Cassie's voice was calm, but filled with emotion. "Besides, I have so much to do."

DeeDee watched her remove a pen and a folded sheet of hotel notepaper from the pocket of her robe. The page, which Cassie opened flat on her lap, contained a list of names and bullet points in her precise handwriting. Reading it upside down, DeeDee was able to decipher what she thought said Order of Service, Hymns, Hair, Catering, and Flowers. One name was crossed off of the top, and

Cassie drew a line through another name, which DeeDee assumed was Wayne.

"I called Dorothy, Johnny's assistant," Cassie trilled. "I felt so bad for her. No one had thought to let her know, and of course she hadn't been able to get ahold of Johnny all day. It was such a shock for the woman. She was totally distraught after I told her. I hope she's okay."

DeeDee knew Cassie's chatter was her way of coping with her grief, but it was unnerving to hear her proceed to rattle down the shopping list of things to buy for his funeral, including a new dress, before stopping to ask DeeDee whether she thought a hat was appropriate.

"Cassie...I'm not sure about the hat, but there's something else I'd like to run past you, if that's okay," DeeDee said, reaching over and gently taking the paper and pen from Cassie's hands.

"Do you mind if I tell Jake what you said earlier about Greg? And I'm glad you told me about Wayne and the restrictive covenant in the trust fund, because if it turns out that Johnny didn't die from natural causes, I think identifying anyone who might have had a grudge against Johnny will be important."

Cassie's eyes were glassy. "You mean Greg isn't the only one who might have wanted to kill Johnny?"

"We don't know if anyone killed Johnny, but say someone did. Jake's a private investigator, and he knows a lot about motives. It sounds like Wayne would have a motive as well as Greg. I don't want you to worry about all of this. You have enough going on what with everything that needs to happen when a family member passes away."

"Okay," Cassie said, reaching for the paper and taking it out of DeeDee's hand. "I think telling Jake is a good idea. I'm just going to lie down for a few minutes, and then I'll finish my list." She leaned back on the bed and closed her eyes.

DeeDee waited until she was sure Cassie was asleep, and then tip-toed over to place a blanket on her tiny frame. A faint smile was visible on Cassie's lips, and DeeDee knew she was dreaming of Johnny.

CHAPTER FIFTEEN

The overcast sky reflected the somber mood in the car when DeeDee and Jake drove back to Seattle the following morning. Even Balto seemed to sense the gravity of the situation, and he laid down quietly in the back seat without having to be told.

"Cassie told me she and her children were leaving first thing this morning," DeeDee said. "The coroner told her he'd be in touch with her as soon as there is any news, and then the funeral company will take Johnny's body back to Mercer Island."

"I hope the body can be released soon," Jake said. "This has to be a very stressful situation for the family, although it sounds like Cassie is dealing fairly well with everything."

"Too well," DeeDee said. "I don't think the reality of Johnny's death has hit her yet."

They sped along the mountain highway, the spectacular view of Howe Sound filtered by the grainy white morning mist. DeeDee watched Jake's strong arms holding the wheel steady and glanced up at his serious face.

When she'd returned from Cassie's room the previous evening, she'd told Jake about her conversation with Briana, and what Cassie had told her about Greg Baker, as well the details of the phone call

94

with Wayne. Now, she voiced the thoughts that had been running through her head all night.

"Jake, do you think Johnny was murdered?"

He glanced over at DeeDee, his face grim. "Do you really want to know?"

The radio was on, and DeeDee leaned forward to turn the music down. She nodded.

"Looks to me like the odds are stacking up that way," Jake said. "Considering what's come out of the woodwork since Johnny died, I'd say there's a good chance there was more than nature at work when it comes to examining the cause of his death. Everyone said he was a health nut, and his physician recently checked him over before he started marathon training and gave him the go-ahead for it. What do we know so far about anyone who might have been gunning for him?"

"There's Mimi Edmonds," DeeDee said, "the woman who Briana said had been calling Johnny. All we know is that she worked for him, and it sounds like she'd been stalking him or they were having an affair."

"Seems like more than a crush," Jake said, "based on the phone conversation Briana overheard when she and Johnny were at Starbucks. What else have we got?"

"Greg Baker," DeeDee continued, "He's the man who was in love with Cassie a long time ago and possibly ever since. We know he wanted to meet Johnny in Whistler, and Cassie and Johnny argued about it the night before he died. Cassie was against the meeting taking place, and she's convinced he's involved somehow."

"I met Greg briefly yesterday morning," Jake said. "Clark introduced us."

"What was he like?" DeeDee asked.

Jake thought for a moment. "Insipid sort of guy with a floppy handshake and a weaselly looking goatee. Looked like an accountant or something."

"Hey, my son's an accountant," DeeDee protested.

"Just kidding," Jake said with a smile. "You must have mentioned that, and I just slipped it in to pull your chain." He signaled to change lanes. "Or maybe I can spot a bean counter at fifty paces."

DeeDee rolled her eyes. "You haven't met Mitch yet. Let's move on. Next up is Wayne Roberts, Johnny's younger brother. He's a down-and-out loser with a love for the high life, but his trust fund was controlled by Johnny. According to Cassie, he has a low moral code and is desperate for money. With Johnny out of the way, he gets full access to all of his trust fund cash. After talking to him, it wouldn't surprise me if he's waiting outside Cassie's house when she arrives home today, so he can get his hands on the money."

"Okay," Jake said. "When we stop for coffee I'll call my assistant, Rob, and have him run some background checks on Wayne Roberts, Mimi Edmonds, Greg Baker, and Derek Adams. He should be able to have some preliminary information for us by the time we get back to Bainbridge Island."

One of the names was unfamiliar to DeeDee. "Wait a minute," she said. "Who's Derek Adams? I don't think I've heard his name before."

"Ah," Jake said. "Sorry, I didn't get a chance to tell you. Derek is the golf pro at the Island View Golf Club. A man called Ray Wentworth overheard me telling some of the other men that I'm a private investigator and you're a friend of the Roberts' family. He said he thought I should know about a heated argument Johnny was involved in at the golf club about a week ago."

DeeDee looked over at Jake. "Really? I can't see Johnny picking an argument, but knowing him, I don't think he'd back down from one if he was challenged."

"From what Ray told me, Johnny was taunting Derek about beating him in a golf game, and said he could do it again at Whistler," Jake said. "Also, Derek said he thought Johnny was trying to get him fired, and Johnny retorted by saying Derek was already going about it the right way. Apparently, Derek swore that Johnny would be sorry for saying that. There were several witnesses who saw and heard it all."

DeeDee sucked in her breath. "That doesn't sound good. Did you meet Derek?"

Jake shook his head. "No. Ray told me Derek was booked for the trip, but he hadn't seen him. I took a quick look at the registration list for the tournament, and Derek's name had been crossed off. When I casually mentioned it to the young man at the registration desk, he said Derek had called the club earlier to cancel."

"Do you think he changed his mind about playing because he was worried Johnny might beat him again?" DeeDee asked.

"Possibly," Jake said. He drummed his fingers on the steering wheel, checked the rear-view mirror, and abruptly changed lanes. "I think we should get Rob on this sooner rather than later." He pulled the car off at the next exit and stopped in front of a small doughnut shop. "Unplanned coffee stop. You get the coffee while I make the call to Rob. Let's wait and see what he comes back with. This should keep him busy for a while."

*****

It was late afternoon when they arrived back at DeeDee's home on Bainbridge Island. DeeDee stretched her legs while Jake carried her luggage inside. She threw some of Balto's toys into the garden, and Balto ran after them. He chased them and then began to wrestle in the grass with his toy rabbit.

DeeDee followed Jake inside, and stepped around the large black suitcase in the hallway. The light on her answering machine was flashing.

"I'll call you as soon as I hear anything from Rob," Jake said, smoothing her hair. He tilted her chin upward and leaned down for a gentle kiss. DeeDee closed her eyes, and Jake's lips skimmed hers with a light touch that she knew would linger in her mind long after he was gone.

"Get some rest," Jake said as he left. "It's been a stressful couple of days, and I have a feeling it's not over yet."

DeeDee watched Jake get into his truck and drive away before she walked into the kitchen. She looked at the meager contents of the refrigerator and made a mental note that a trip to the supermarket was definitely in order. She'd shopped a week ago, but deliberately hadn't gotten groceries before she left. She didn't want everything to be spoiled when she returned. By the time she'd showered, changed clothes, made coffee, and opened her mail, it was a far more relaxed DeeDee who pressed the button on her answering machine to pick up her messages.

There were a couple of messages about catering bookings for Deelish, the message she'd missed from Roz about the change in accommodation plans for Whistler, and finally, an hysterical message which was hard to decipher. DeeDee's hand shook as she rewound the machine to play it again.

A high-pitched recorded voice filled the hallway. "DeeDee? It's Cassie. Are you there, DeeDee? Please call me as soon as you get home." If the person hadn't said it was Cassie, DeeDee wouldn't have recognized her voice at all. Cassie, who was normally quiet and soft-spoken, had sounded loud, shrill, and very upset.

DeeDee lifted the receiver and dialed Cassie's home number, which she knew by heart. Cassie answered immediately, making DeeDee suspect she must have been sitting beside the phone or else holding it in her hand. In her mind's eye, DeeDee could imagine Cassie pacing back and forth on the marble kitchen floor of her large home on Mercer Island.

"DeeDee, is that you?" Cassie shrieked when she answered the phone.

"Yes, I just picked up your message. What is it Cassie, what's wrong?" It was clear to DeeDee that something was very wrong indeed.

Between Cassie's heaving sobs and the sound of Briana trying to soothe her in the background, DeeDee could just barely make out what Cassie was trying to say.

"Poison, DeeDee," Cassie said. "The coroner thinks Johnny was poisoned. Can you help me DeeDee, please? I think I've lost it. I can't cope with making the funeral arrangements, writing the obituary, and getting the house ready. I'm at the end of my rope. Please, can you come over?" she wailed. "The children are doing the best they can, but they're as devastated as I am."

"I'll be there tomorrow," DeeDee promised. "Please, Cassie, don't worry about any of those things. I'll take care of them. Try to keep calm. I'll see you tomorrow around noon, okay?"

There was mumbling and choked crying coming from the other end of the line, then DeeDee heard Briana's voice speaking quietly.

"DeeDee, Mom can't talk any more. If you could come over from Bainbridge tomorrow, we'd all appreciate it. I'm worried about Mom. I've never seen her like this. You could probably tell from talking to her that she isn't coping well at all."

DeeDee assured Briana she'd be there the next day following an appointment she had in the morning. From what she'd just heard, like Briana, she was worried about Cassie too, but not surprised that Cassie had finally cracked under the pressure. The news about Johnny hadn't sunk in the day before, but now the gravity of what had happened had gotten through to her, loud and clear.

DeeDee lifted a jacket from the coat rack and went out to the front deck, closing the door behind her. "Let's go for a walk, Balto," she called across the garden. She needed to feel the ocean breeze on her face. So what if it messed up her hair, if it would help clear her troubled mind, that was a small price to pay. Clipping the leash onto Balto's collar, she led him on a brisk walk down the path towards the beach.

Balto ran in and out of the gentle ocean waves lapping at the beach, and DeeDee let the wind wash over her body and quiet her mind. The walks she shared with Balto on the beach at Bainbridge Island were like a form of therapy for her. She'd never attended therapy sessions in the past, but there were many times when she thought it would have been helpful, particularly when Lyle had told her he was leaving her for a younger woman.

She thought about how her life had changed over the past year, and how Cassie's world had been upended in the space of a few moments. When the funeral was over, she thought she'd invite Cassie to spend some time with her on Bainbridge Island. Maybe Cassie would find the beach walks as therapeutic as DeeDee did. In the meantime, DeeDee was happy to go and stay with Cassie on Mercer Island for as long as she was needed.

She decided to take a pot roast she'd slow cooked and frozen before she'd left for Whistler with her. She doubted that food was a very high priority for Cassie right now. First though, there was one stop she'd decided she was going to make on her way to Cassie's the following morning. J.R. Mercedes was on the way to Cassie's home, and there was someone there DeeDee wanted to meet.

CHAPTER SIXTEEN

"Looks like you're my date for tonight, Balto."

DeeDee was relaxing in one of the chairs on the outside deck, Balto lying at her feet. Instead of the planned getaway to Whistler, she found herself on a Sunday night at 9:00 p.m. in the company of a husky dog, a glass of Sauvignon Blanc, and a bowl of nachos. She was exhausted after the events of the last two days, and the bubble bath she'd taken when they came back from the beach to help her relax was making her sleepy.

Just when she was contemplating whether to call it a night or to replenish the nachos, her cell phone rang and Jake's name flashed up on the screen. She reached down to the side table, lifted up the phone, and tapped the glass to accept the call.

"Hey, DeeDee," Jake said, the deep timbre of his voice causing a warm tingle to travel down her spine. She wished he was there with her, instead of at the other end of the line.

"Hey, yourself," she said. Her voice was the only sound in the still, evening darkness. The light on the deck came from the faint glow visible from a table lamp inside the living room. She loved the peace and quiet of her new home on Bainbridge Island. She was close enough to other nearby houses to feel safe, but her location allowed her to have plenty of privacy. "I spoke to Cassie earlier. It's not good news, I'm afraid. The coroner's tests indicate Johnny was poisoned."

There was a long pause on the other end of the line while Jake digested the news. "I'm not really surprised," Jake said when he finally spoke up. "Considering how health-conscious Johnny was, it would be more of a shock if he'd died from natural causes, however I'll let Inspector Stewart know, if he doesn't already."

"Thanks Jake," DeeDee said, swirling the wine around in her glass before taking a sip. "What do you think will happen next?"

"If it's a murder investigation, Inspector Stewart will probably have to come down here, since that's where all the persons of interest are likely to be. I suppose there could be some other suspects we don't know about, but Rob's come up with some very interesting information about the ones we were talking about earlier."

DeeDee was pretty sure Jake had been working right alongside Rob to investigate Johnny's death from the time he'd gotten home from Whistler.

"What did Rob find?" DeeDee asked.

"First of all, he spoke to the manager of Island View Golf Club," Jake said, "and explained Cassie was using a private investigator in case it turned out Johnny didn't die of natural causes. Rob said he was gathering as much background information as possible about Johnny's various business and social relationships and wondered if the manager could tell him about the Whistler trip or anything else that might be relevant."

"I see," DeeDee said. "Did the manager have much to say?"

"Just that about twenty of them went on the golf trip," Jake began. "It was an all-male group, and a mix of ages. He said the group consisted of members that play together regularly. Johnny had been a member of the club for years, and everyone knew he took his position as president of the Men's Golf Excursions very seriously. The group was really looking forward to this year's trip because

Johnny always made sure it had a personal touch. He spoke highly of Johnny and said they would all miss him," Jake added.

"Oh," DeeDee said, "that's nice. Did he mention anything about Derek Adams?"

"Patience, DeeDee," Jake said with a laugh. "I'm just getting to that part. Rob asked if the golf pro went on the trip. The manager confirmed what they had told me at the Chateau Fairmont Golf Course on the day of the tournament, that Derek Adams was a no-show. Evidently he was planning on going, but something personal came up at the last minute and he said he couldn't make it. Rob found out that Derek lives in the Sunrise Apartments on Mercer Island with his girlfriend, Annette Lewis."

"I know exactly where that is," DeeDee said. "When Mitch was a young boy, one of his friends lived there. I used to spend a lot of time driving over there to take him and pick him up from sleepovers."

Sunrise Apartments was not the most desirable address, but it was one of the few places on the island where the rents were reasonable. DeeDee remembered that Mitch's friend was the best video game player at their school, and she heard he'd gone on to become a YouTube gamer millionaire, so it was pretty unlikely he'd still be living there.

"Rob also did some digging on Mimi," Jake continued. "He found out that Ms. Edmonds has had relationships with several wealthy men in the Seattle area. She apparently met them when they bought cars from her. It would start with a test drive, then she'd keep in touch with them as part of the follow-up service. You can figure out the rest."

"Hmm. So that's what they're calling it these days," DeeDee said with a chuckle, "follow-up service, what a convenient term."

"Rob talked to the General Manager of Johnny's dealership," Jake went on. "He said it was pretty well known that Mimi had a thing for

Johnny. It seems, however, that Johnny was the last one to catch on. Or if he knew about it, his way of dealing with it was to simply ignore it."

"I can imagine Johnny would do that rather than feeding the monster," DeeDee confirmed. "That sounds about right."

"Recently though, Mimi started doing what the manager called one step away from stalking Johnny. Apparently Mimi and Johnny had a pretty intense conversation at their last sales review meeting. It appears Mimi's days off last week were Friday and Saturday, the day Johnny was killed. She rotates Saturdays, but she always works on Sundays, because that's when she makes the most sales."

"I see," DeeDee said, as she thought that Mimi Edmonds sounded like a real piece of work. "And what about the two others, Wayne and Greg? Did Rob find anything out about them?"

"He sure did," Jake said. "Wayne, Johnny's loser brother, lives in a rundown part of Seattle. He's behind on his rent and owes money to various people at a seedy bar, Fat Al's, which he frequents on a daily basis. He doesn't work, and he lives off the allowance from the trust fund that Johnny controlled. He's been arrested a couple of times for minor infractions and misdemeanors. Johnny always came to his rescue and paid for a lawyer to defend him."

"Oh," DeeDee said, shocked. Now it made even more sense why she'd never heard Wayne's name mentioned in the Roberts' household.

"Rob spoke to Wayne's neighbor, who said Wayne had been away for a few days, but he'd returned Saturday night. They said it wasn't unusual for him to be gone for several days, since he only came home when the latest woman he'd picked up got tired of him and kicked him out."

"Ugh," DeeDee said. "I really don't look forward to meeting him. He sounds disgusting. What about Greg Baker? I hope at least he's got some redeeming qualities."

"I guess Cassie thought so once," Jake said, "even if she's since changed her mind. Okay, business-wise, Greg has been moderately successful. He has his own accounting practice, but he's not a big-league player. His personal life has been more checkered. He's been divorced three times. The first divorce wasn't all that long after he wanted Cassie to leave Johnny for him"

"Sounds like a rebound marriage," DeeDee observed. "What's also interesting is that Cassie said at the time that she was attracted to him one of the reasons was that he was rock solid. Doesn't look like that was a very good assessment of his character."

"You're probably right," Jake agreed. "His first marriage lasted a grand total of seventy-four days. The next two were longer. His second wife was a barmaid, and the third was a blackjack dealer at one of the Indian casinos north of Seattle. He has a total of five children by his second and third wives. From what Rob found out, his spousal support and child support payments eat up most of his disposable income. The employees at his office, according to what Rob found out on social media, say they're underpaid, and that he's lecherous and a sexist."

"Wow," DeeDee said. "Rob's thorough, I'll say that much. I'm sure glad Cassie didn't run off with him, but I am surprised she was ever attracted to him at all. From what you've told me, it seems Greg was the only one of the suspects that was in Whistler when Johnny was murdered. Maybe Cassie's hunch about Greg killing Johnny is correct."

"Not so fast, Watson," Jake said. "We still don't know where the other three were. Any of them could have been in Whistler without us knowing about it. Rob's still working on that angle, so we're really not in a position to draw any conclusions just yet. I'm going to pass all of the information Rob found out on to Inspector Stewart in the morning and see if the police in Whistler have come up with anything locally. Why don't you sleep on it, and we'll catch up again tomorrow?"

"Okay," DeeDee said, with a smile. "Thanks for all of your help with this, Jake. I know Cassie will really appreciate it. She was very upset when we spoke, so I'm going over to her home on Mercer Island tomorrow and see what I can do to help her out."

"That's awfully nice of you," Jake said.

"It's what friends do," DeeDee replied. "Cassie was there for me when Lyle left, and she would be again in a heartbeat. We can count on each other."

"Yes," Jake said. "We can."

DeeDee knew that comment was directed at her, and that the reason Jake was doing all of this for Cassie was because of his deep feelings for DeeDee. At that moment, her heart felt like it was going to burst with affection for this man who had only been in her life for a short time, but without whom she knew she'd be lost.

"Let's go to bed, Balto," DeeDee said, after she and Jake had said goodnight and ended their call. She locked up and filled Balto's water bowl before turning the table lamp off and heading upstairs.

Her warm, cozy bed was calling to her when her phone buzzed again. Tempted to ignore the incoming call, she hesitated when she saw Roz's name appear on the screen. Setting down her toothbrush, DeeDee swiped the glass on the phone.

CHAPTER SEVENTEEN

During the telephone call with Roz the night before, Roz had said, "Promise me you won't do anything stupid," when DeeDee had told her about her plan to go and see Mimi Edmonds at the J.R. Mercedes dealership, since it was on the way to Cassie's home.

DeeDee had assured her sister she had no intention of doing anything stupid. As she dialed J.R. Mercedes the next morning to make an appointment with Mimi, she didn't think it was stupid at all. If anything, she was congratulating herself on what she thought was an excellent idea. All DeeDee wanted to do was meet the woman who, according to some, had been stalking Johnny Roberts, or close to it, and see for herself what Mimi was like. She'd often heard Johnny boast that the security company he used was the best in the city, so DeeDee considered that a company that viewed all the activity in a high-end dealership with 24/7 security was as safe a place to be as anywhere on a Monday morning.

"I'd like to make an appointment with Mimi Edmonds, please," DeeDee said to the receptionist who answered her call. "I'm looking for a new Mercedes, top of the line, and Ms. Edmonds has been recommended to me by several friends."

DeeDee could hear the receptionist clicking on her computer keyboard. "I'm sorry," the female voice replied. "Mimi has no available appointments today. She's fully booked. Would you be available Wednesday, instead?"

DeeDee thought for a second. "That's a shame," she said. "I leave tomorrow for an extended vacation in the Caribbean, and I really wanted to order the car before I left. I'm going to need some help choosing the extra custom upgrades I want. Silly me, I should have called earlier. I suppose I can go to another dealership, but thanks for your help."

"Wait," the woman said, her clicking becoming frantic. "Ryan Connell could see you today, or…"

"Never mind," DeeDee said. "The person who recommended Mimi to me is a friend of the Roberts' family, and he said I should only deal with Mimi. Maybe next time. Both of my children are getting new cars soon, so I might try again then." She paused. "Thank you and goodbye…"

"I just realized Mimi has a cancellation for 12:30 this afternoon," the receptionist interrupted.

"That's perfect," DeeDee said. "Thank you. That will work for me."

It meant she wouldn't arrive at Cassie's until a little later than planned, but she'd call Cassie on the way and explain. DeeDee dressed in a casual outfit of cropped fitted pants, a light linen knit over a silk blouse, and flats. She carefully applied her makeup, blow-dried her hair, and spritzed herself with a liberal dose of Michael Kors fragrance. She decided on her Coach purse, and then checked herself over in the mirror.

Balto watched her fix a smudge of mascara on her eyelid, his head tilted to one side, with a quizzical look on his face.

"Do you think I look as if I'm about to buy a $70,000 car, Balto?" DeeDee asked. "Well, if you won't answer me, I just hope I can convince Mimi. C'mon, let's go."

Balto obediently followed DeeDee out to her SUV. She loaded a small suitcase containing some overnight things into it, the roast she'd taken out of the freezer and had in a cooler with ice, a dog bed, and some dog food for Balto, since she wasn't sure how long they'd be gone. When everything was loaded into the car, including Balto in the back seat, she went back inside to get her purse and lock up. When she returned to the car moments later, Balto had moved up to the front seat.

DeeDee laughed. "Okay, Balto. You can ride shotgun with me today. Hopefully we won't get into any trouble."

*****

As usual, Balto enjoyed the ferry ride from Bainbridge Island to Seattle. The boat wasn't busy, and DeeDee bumped into her friend Tammy on the ferry. She had her dog, Buddy, with her. The thirty-five-minute ride was just long enough for DeeDee to briefly fill Tammy in about the drama on the trip to Whistler, while Balto and Buddy played on the passenger deck.

"I promise I'll stop by the cafe when we get back from Cassie's house," DeeDee said, before they made their way to their cars when the boat was close to the dock at the Seattle terminal. "I need to see Susie anyway."

"You better stop by," Tammy said, waving them off. "Be careful. I don't need to remind you that you have a knack for getting mixed up with murders."

DeeDee thought about Tammy's comment as she drove through the streets of Seattle on the way to J.R. Mercedes. She tried to convince herself that the fact she'd found herself caught up in two murder investigations in the past six months was just bad luck. She couldn't imagine it was something that would ever happen again. If she could just help Cassie through this one, DeeDee was sure she would never have to do any more amateur sleuthing for the rest of her life.

"Here we are, Balto," DeeDee said as she parked outside the J.R. Mercedes showroom just before 12:30. Her SUV looked pretty shabby compared to the shiny cars that were for sale and parked in the display lot. Even the used cars looked brand new. Balto wanted to get out of the SUV, and he started pawing at the door handle.

"Sorry, big guy," DeeDee said firmly. "You have to stay in the car." She ignored Balto's whines and rolled the window down far enough to allow him to get plenty of fresh air. "I'll be back soon, I promise."

As she walked over to the glass-enclosed showroom, DeeDee stopped and admired a few of the used vehicles on display that she passed along the way. She had to remind herself she wasn't really car shopping. She was just role-playing and trying to get a sense of Mimi. Even so, it was fun to pretend.

Inside the airy and bright showroom, a friendly young woman at the reception desk greeted DeeDee and wrote down some information. "Mimi will be with you in just a moment, Mrs. Wilson," the receptionist assured her. "Please, take a seat." Her arm gestured toward an area with black leather and chrome Barcelona chairs, surrounded by tall, leafy green potted plants.

DeeDee wondered if the plants were real, since they looked almost too convincing. She was about to reach out and touch one of the leaves when the receptionist asked, "May I get you some coffee?"

"No, I'm fine, thank you," DeeDee said, smiling, her arm dropping back to her side. She remained standing, looking around. Several salesmen dressed in well-tailored suits were talking to customers on the showroom floor. They stood beside the latest Mercedes models, some with their doors open. Signs beside the cars showed the retail price and alternative leasing options. The entire place was shiny and sparkling, from the cars, to the glass exterior windows, to the glass-walled offices in the interior of the building. It smelled of money and that new car smell which DeeDee wished she could buy in an aerosol can and spray in her own three-year old SUV.

The click of Mimi's stiletto heels on the marble floor signaled her arrival before she came into view from around the side of a black

Mercedes sedan. DeeDee had no doubt that the stunningly gorgeous blond woman sashaying towards her was Mimi Edmonds. Several of the other customers in the showroom also turned to stare at her hourglass figure and long legs that went on for miles before reaching a thigh-skimming skirt into which she'd tucked a low-cut blouse. On anyone else the outfit might have made them look like a streetwalker, but Mimi owned the look.

Her picture-perfect face was framed by sleek golden tresses with caramel and platinum highlights. She glowed, and it wasn't just her hair and skin. The chunky diamonds she wore on her ears, wrists, and nestled in between what DeeDee thought were her best assets, although it was a tough call, considering everything else Mimi had going for her, created a dazzling display to complete the package.

DeeDee was dumbstruck. The woman looked amazing, and there was no doubt she knew it. As Mimi greeted her with a gleaming smile and walked over to her, DeeDee noticed she was wearing what looked like Jimmy Choo shoes. DeeDee regretted her own choice of comfortable footwear and felt completely dowdy in comparison to this woman who looked like a movie star.

"Mrs. Wilson, how lovely to meet you," Mimi said, extending her hand, which DeeDee shook with trepidation. She suspected Mimi was aware of the effect she had on people, and no doubt would try to use it to her advantage in car sales negotiations. Since DeeDee had no intention of buying anything, she told herself she had nothing to fear. "I'm so happy to be able to help you today," Mimi purred. "Why don't we step into my office?"

DeeDee followed Mimi into an impressive office with two dark wooden desks, one on either side of the room. Mimi's name was on one, and the other desk, which was unoccupied, had a man's name on it. A liquor cabinet against one wall held what looked like a fully-stocked bar with a row of crystal decanters on top. Mimi shut the glass door to the showroom behind them and motioned for DeeDee to have a seat.

As DeeDee did so, she looked at the framed photographs on the wall behind Mimi's desk. There were several of Mimi at car shows and receiving awards, but DeeDee's gaze paused on a large picture of Johnny Roberts, beaming down at her. DeeDee felt herself choke up. Johnny looked just like she remembered him. Big, grinning, and happy.

"Is that Johnny Roberts?" she asked Mimi. "I heard he died recently."

Mimi's eyes narrowed as she watched DeeDee. "Yes, he was my boss. Did you know him?"

"Oh, no," DeeDee said, pulling her eyes away from Johnny's photograph. She forced herself to make eye contact with Mimi. "He was an acquaintance of a friend of mine who recommended that I come here." She glanced up at the wall again. "He certainly was attractive. It looks like he had tremendous presence."

"Depends on who you talk to, I suppose," Mimi said with a laugh. "He was great at selling cars, and he was a good boss, but I hear he was a lousy husband."

DeeDee tried to look casual. "Really? What makes you say that?"

Mimi glanced toward the door before leaning across the table. "His marriage was a sham. Johnny was chasing after every piece of skirt in town. I used to feel sorry for his wife. I'm sure his death is a blessing for her. Maybe her next husband will have more respect for her than Johnny did."

"That's terrible," DeeDee said, "and his wife knew nothing about it?"

"Oh, no," Mimi said, with a conspiratorial smile. She suddenly stopped herself. "I'm so sorry. I forgot your friend knows the family. I really shouldn't say anything else, out of respect for the dead. What's done is done. I just hope his wife never finds out what he was like. Letting her continue to believe the lie would probably be the kindest thing to do under the circumstances."

DeeDee felt her cheeks redden at Mimi's words. The man she was describing did not sound at all like the Johnny she'd known. She looked at Mimi, and in an instant, she saw right through her. Everything about her was fake. Her hair extensions, her teeth, her breasts, and most of all, her lies about Johnny. DeeDee decided she didn't need to sit through one more second of this woman's mean-spiritedness. She'd learned everything she needed to know about Mimi Edmonds.

DeeDee suddenly realized that Mimi had continued talking and was now staring at her, waiting for a reply. She had no idea what Mimi had said. "Um, I…"

"The car, Mrs. Wilson? I understand you want to finalize your order today. What model do you have in mind?"

DeeDee didn't appreciate the fact that Mimi was looking at her like she was some kind of an idiot. She bet Mimi treated her male customers in a completely different way.

Regaining her composure, DeeDee took a sheet of paper from her purse. She'd gone online that morning and had copied down the specifications for her dream convertible Mercedes sports car. "It's a Mercedes SLC convertible. Black metallic, leather seats, premium extra package. I've written it all down." She pushed the sheet of paper across the desk to Mimi, whose expression suddenly turned friendlier.

DeeDee abruptly stood up. She couldn't take being with this woman for another moment. "I've just realized I'm not going to have time for a test-drive today. If you could call me with the price this afternoon, we can finalize the payment details. My contact information is all there."

"Do you require financing, Mrs. Wilson, or will you be taking the leasing option?"

DeeDee gave Mimi a horrified look. "Goodness, no," she said, with a flick of her arm. "I'll pay cash."

Mimi scrambled to open the door for her, and DeeDee left smiling through gritted teeth. She hoped Mimi would have fun later on when she called the fake number she'd written on the paper which was for a fast-food restaurant in downtown Seattle.

*****

Mimi closed the door to her office and sat down to write up DeeDee's contract. A moment later her cell phone rang, and she saw her son's name on the monitor.

"Hi, Josh. From what I've seen in the media it looks like your trip to Whistler was a success. How did you like the private plane and staying at the Fairmont Chateau?"

"Mom, the plane ride was amazing. That's beautiful country, and I've never stayed in anything like the Fairmont, but there's something I have to tell you."

"And what is that?" Mimi asked.

"Well, I got to thinking about what would happen to me if anyone ever discovered that I was the one who'd poisoned the guy you told me about. I actually had the ricin in my pocket when I went up to his room, and I was going to put it in his coffee just liked we talked about, but at the last minute I couldn't do it. I even delivered the coffee to him and pretended I was with room service.

"Man, you would have been so proud of me. I mean I nailed the look of someone delivering room service. Getting the coat and everything else was pretty easy, but then I realized I don't ever want to go back to prison. The coffee I gave him was just that, coffee. I let you down and I'm sorry, but I just couldn't do it. I know you probably won't understand, but from what I hear someone else did it, so maybe the whole thing was just meant to be."

Mimi was quiet for a moment and then she said, "So, if you didn't do it, I wonder who did?"

"Mom, I have no idea. I gotta go. Guess my life's beginning to turn around. Believe it or not, I've got an interview for a job, and I don't want to mess it up by being late. Talk to you later."

After her call from Josh ended, Mimi sat at her desk for a long time, wondering who killed Johnny Roberts. She wasn't the only one who wondered.

CHAPTER EIGHTEEN

Just one more quick stop, DeeDee thought when she arrived on Mercer Island.

She felt like she'd handled the meeting with Mimi very well, and the idea to see if anyone was home at the Sunrise Apartment building where Derek Adams and Annette Lewis lived had just occurred to her. In the back of her mind DeeDee had a nagging thought that no one knew she was going there, which was a bad idea in case something happened to her. But she told herself that she had Balto, and she was only going in the apartment house for a minute or two. Then she would go straight to Cassie's home without any more detours. The streets near the apartment building were still familiar to DeeDee, and she easily found a parking space.

"Okay Balto, we're going for a little walk now," she said. Balto jumped out as soon as she opened the door. "I need to make a quick visit somewhere."

She gave Balto some water and waited while he drank it, then she locked the car door, and the two of them walked towards the Sunrise Apartment building. It was a quiet Monday afternoon, and a light wind was blowing leaves across the sidewalk which was deserted except for Balto and her. Since it was Monday, and the people living in the apartment were more than likely working people, she was worried no one would be home.

When they arrived at the shabby building, there was a "No Dogs" sign hanging prominently on the gate at the entrance to the building. She thought for a moment and said, "We'd better not draw attention for getting ejected by the apartment manager or an angry tenant, Balto. I'm going to have to take you back to the car."

The nagging thought in the back of DeeDee's mind had become a voice and was getting louder by the time she'd made the round trip to the car and back. Standing in front of the apartment building without Balto, she couldn't stop herself from thinking about what the outcome might be if Derek became angry. She couldn't rely on Balto for help, although if she didn't return to the car soon, she wouldn't put it past him to start barking and alert people there might be a problem.

What would Jake tell me to do? she thought. She could hear his voice saying '*Get out of there right now.*'

Hesitating before pushing on the creaky gate, she knew the sensible thing to do would be to turn around and forget the whole thing. She pressed ahead regardless, telling herself there was no reason to be afraid, even though her heart felt like it was about to pound right out of her chest. She hoped there was a directory of tenants inside the building, or she'd have to start knocking on random doors. She didn't want to hang around this place any longer than was necessary.

Once she was inside the building she found herself in a dreary hallway that was dark and forbidding with no sunshine in spite of the name of the apartment building. DeeDee was glad to see a list of the tenants and their apartment numbers next to the elevator. She noted the information she needed ad then stepped around a shallow pool of unidentified liquid to enter the elevator. On the ride up to the fourth floor, she couldn't help but notice the traces of graffiti written on the walls, which cleaning had been unable to erase.

When DeeDee got out of the elevator, there was even more evidence of why this wasn't considered to be one of the better apartments on the island. The stench of blocked sewer drains hit her, intermingled with cooking smells, and a trace of stale cigarette smoke. She thought the place could definitely do with a renovation to its plumbing and air-conditioning systems, preferably something that filtered the unpleasant odors.

DeeDee knocked on the door of apartment 4e and waited. She thought she could hear someone crying softly inside the apartment, and she moved closer to the door.

"Hello?" she said in a loud voice, her face as close to the door as she could get it without banging her nose on the splintered wood. "Is anyone home?"

The crying stopped for a moment, and then a woman's tear-filled voice called out, "Who is it?"

"My name is DeeDee Wilson. My friend's husband died recently when he was on a golf trip to Whistler. He was a member of the Island View Golf Club. I'll only take a moment of your time, but I wonder if you could help me." DeeDee waited in anticipation, but there was no response. "Please? I really want to talk to you."

DeeDee's head was bowed, and she noticed that some of the brown liquid from downstairs had seeped onto her gray Italian leather shoes. She shook her foot in dismay.

The door opened a crack, and then a little more, until DeeDee was face-to-face with a small woman who appeared to be in her twenties. Her eyes were red and swollen, and she was holding a Kleenex up to her nose. Her messy brown hair was pulled back off a pretty face which had several raw patches of eczema. She was dressed in sweats and slippers, and DeeDee noticed her hands and lower arms were also covered with red and white patches of flaky skin.

"I'm sorry for disturbing you," she said to the young woman, who regarded her through narrowed eyes. "It looks like I've caught you at a bad time."

"S'ok," the woman said, opening the door wide enough for

DeeDee to enter. "I'm sorry about your friend. I'm Annette Lewis."

She motioned for DeeDee to enter the plainly furnished apartment. The smell of antiseptic and bleach in the room stung DeeDee's eyes and tickled her throat. She swallowed. There was a kitchen dinette area on one side of the room, and a living area on the other which had a small couch, a coffee table, and an arm chair on the other. A glass of water and several white medicine bottles were on the kitchen counter alongside a cleaning rag.

"Please, have a seat," Annette said with a tight smile. DeeDee sat on the sofa while Annette sat on the edge of the arm chair beside it.

"Derek isn't here right now. It's very nice of you to come and visit me."

It occurred to DeeDee that Annette was sick, and that maybe she'd misunderstood the reason for DeeDee's visit.

"That's okay," DeeDee said. "My friend's name was Johnny Roberts. The coroner thinks he was poisoned. Did you or Derek know him?"

"Please excuse the apartment," Annette said, ignoring DeeDee's question. "The place is a mess. I wasn't expecting company."

DeeDee looked around. The place was spotless. There was nothing out of place, and judging from the smell, DeeDee had no doubt that everything in the apartment was white glove clean.

"I had some treatments last week," Annette sniffed, rubbing her nose with the Kleenex. "Trauma therapy. It was for an incident…well, it happened a long time ago. I'm afraid it's released so many emotions that I can't stop crying. I'm not usually like this at all. Right now, I'm afraid to even go outside."

"I'm sorry to hear that," DeeDee said, her heart going out to Annette. At first glance she looked sad and broken, but somewhere behind the vacant gaze, DeeDee suspected there was a strong woman waiting to emerge.

"Good for you, for taking the steps necessary to deal with those issues," DeeDee said. "That takes a lot of courage. Now, getting back to what I was saying about my friend, I just wondered if you might have heard anything?"

Annette nodded. "I've heard the name Johnny Roberts before. I don't think he was nice to Derek." She reached for a long strand of hair hanging beside her ear, twisted it round her finger and placed it between her lips, chewing on the hair as she spoke. "I remember Derek came home from work one day and said he'd been in a terrible argument with that Johnny man. He said Johnny was always getting to him by talking about how much better he was at golf than Derek."

Annette let the lock of hair fall from her mouth and shook her head from side to side. "That's not true. Derek is the club's pro, and he's the best golfer there. He's just had a lot on his mind lately, and I'm sure that's what the problem was with his game."

"Sure," DeeDee said, trying to placate Annette. She didn't want to be the cause of her crying again.

"I don't think Derek even knows about Johnny's death," Annette said. "I believe he would have said something to me. It sounds very sad."

"Yes, it is," DeeDee said, nodding.

"I'm know Derek wouldn't have wanted anything bad to happen to him," Annette said, playing with her hair again. She sat there smiling at DeeDee with an innocent, angelic look, on her face. Just then there was a knock at the door, and Annette's head turned towards it with a jerk.

"It's me, Louise Higgins," DeeDee heard a woman say from the hallway. Annette got up slowly, and walked over to the door. When she opened it, DeeDee saw the woman standing in the hallway hand Annette a casserole dish.

"I heard Derek leave for work this morning," Louise said. "I'm glad you're feeling better dear, so Derek could go out. He's been so good staying home with you the past few days. I brought you dinner for later."

"Thanks Louise. I haven't felt like cooking," Annette said, shuffling from foot to foot.

"Derek told me he was so worried about your weight loss," Louise said. "I want you to eat all of this and get your strength back, you hear me?" She beamed at Annette and squeezed her arm. Peering inside the door, Louise greeted DeeDee.

"Hello dear, I'm glad Annette has a friend over. She'll be back to her old self in no time."

DeeDee took that as her cue to leave. "I'm sorry, Annette, but I do have to go now. Thank you so much for your help, and I apologize again for bothering you."

"It's no problem," Annette said. "I hope you can come back soon."

DeeDee tiptoed out of the building, carefully avoiding any suspicious wet spots on the floor. Outside, she gasped for fresh air and hurried back to her car. While she was driving to Cassie's house she called Jake to let him know about the conversation with Annette.

"That's one less suspect," Jake said when she was finished. "Seems like Derek has a rock-solid alibi, so that's probably a dead end."

"I think you're right," DeeDee said. "I'm not sure that Annette is the most reliable witness in her current state, but the neighbor would be if she saw Derek there the past few days."

"I think we can cross Mimi off the list as well," Jake said.

"That surprises me." DeeDee hadn't liked Mimi at all, and

wouldn't have minded seeing her spend the rest of her years in an orange prison jumpsuit. Even the thought of that perfect body and face in that outfit made her smile.

"Why's that?" Jake asked.

"Tell you in a minute. You go first."

"Okay," Jake said. "I called the General Manager of J.R. Mercedes to try and get some more information about Mimi. It looks like while she may seem as hard as nails, she also has a soft side to her."

"I didn't see that coming," DeeDee said. "Go on."

"Her grandmother is ninety-six years old," Jake continued. "Mimi pays for her to be taken care of in the most expensive nursing home in Portland. Mimi owns a condo there, and most weeks she goes there on her days off."

DeeDee had a hunch what was coming next. "I suppose the next thing you're going to tell me is that's where she was when Johnny was killed."

"Better than that. I followed up with the nursing home," Jake said. "They confirmed that Mimi visited her grandmother the morning Johnny died. She has an iron clad alibi. That only leaves Johnny's brother and Greg as possible people of interest."

"It sure looks that way based on what we've learned about Derek and Mimi."

"Inspector Stewart is in Seattle to see what he can find out about Wayne. He seems to live a shady life, mostly under the radar. His police team has Greg under surveillance. He came home from Whistler the day golf was canceled, saying he was ill, but so far nothing unusual has turned up on him. Oh, and one more thing, DeeDee."

DeeDee thought Jake sounded stern. "Yes?"

He sighed. "I don't think it was a good idea for you to go to Derek's apartment building without telling me. Please, don't do anything dangerous like that again."

"You don't need to worry," DeeDee assured him. "I was fine." She didn't want to admit how scared she'd been when she entered the building, and how she'd anticipated Jake's disapproval, but ignored it. "Oh, and I have to say I'm surprised about Mimi. That's what I was going to tell you. I met with her earlier as well."

Suddenly, DeeDee didn't feel quite so clever about her meeting with Mimi. She told Jake about her visit to the dealership and how she'd pretended to be interested in ordering a new Mercedes. She noticed that Jake was very quiet while she told him about it.

"DeeDee, in the future when you intend to meet with people of interest in a murder investigation would you please tell me about it beforehand? They might be murderers, you know."

"Ha-ha. I was only trying to help Cassie," she protested meekly.

"I know," Jake said, in a patient tone. "But you can't help anyone if you're dead."

DeeDee was more than happy to listen to Jake's lengthy safety lecture for the rest of her drive to Cassie's. She liked the sound of his voice so much she was willing to put up with it.

CHAPTER NINETEEN

"I'm sorry I'm late," DeeDee said to Cassie. "My appointment took longer than expected."

She embraced her friend, and followed her into a spacious kitchen with beautiful oak cabinets and granite countertops, Balto bringing up the rear.

"Don't worry," Cassie said, pulling out two high stools from the side of the kitchen island. She motioned for DeeDee to have a seat. "We just got back from the mortuary a little while ago, so there would have been no one at home."

DeeDee looked at Cassie with concern. Cassie's petite frame appeared to have shrunk in the two days since DeeDee had seen her. At least she'd regained her composure since the previous afternoon when they had spoken on the phone. Even though Cassie wore a casual blouse, fitted jeans, and ankle boots, DeeDee could tell no thought had gone into her appearance when she'd dressed for the day. She wore no makeup, her cropped hair was slightly tousled, and dark circles hugged eyes that were filled with sorrow. Most of all, DeeDee thought she looked fragile, like she might shatter into pieces at any moment.

"The coroner and the police gave the go-ahead for Johnny's body to be released. It was brought back from Whistler to Seattle this morning," Cassie explained. She poured two glasses of water from the pitcher on the countertop, handing one to DeeDee. "I've decided to have a small, private funeral as soon as possible." Elbows on the counter, Cassie leaned her head on one hand, and closed her eyes for a few moments. When she'd regained her composure, she looked back up at DeeDee. "No fuss. There will be a memorial service later, for his wider circle of friends and business colleagues."

"I think that's a lovely way to handle it."

"The funeral is scheduled for tomorrow," Cassie said. "To change the subject from bad to bad, Johnny's brother called me last night. He's making a terrible fuss about the trust fund money. I'm glad you're here, because he's on his way over right now."

DeeDee squeezed Cassie's hand. "No problem. What is the process for Wayne to get his funds, now that Johnny's deceased?"

Cassie shrugged. "I really don't know. Johnny was the one who dealt with that. I've never even seen the paperwork on it, and I'm not sure where it even is. Johnny had a safe in his office at the dealership, so it might be there."

"Cassie, Wayne can't expect that to be your priority when you have yet to bury your husband. I'm sure he'll understand and be able to wait for a reasonable period of time."

The sudden sound of banging on the front door made her suspect she may have been mistaken about Wayne willing to wait. If that was Wayne, he sounded impatient, very impatient. They heard Briana's voice in the hallway greet whoever had banged on the door, followed by a deep hacking cough that DeeDee had heard before. She and Cassie exchanged looks, before turning in unison to view the disheveled man who walked into the kitchen.

Wayne Roberts was tall, like his brother, but any similarities stopped there. Wayne's face was red, and there was a sheen of perspiration visible on his forehead. His eyes were sunken dark slits above puffy cheeks. The raised veins on his face and his red bulbous nose were clues to his excessive drinking habits. In case there was any doubt, Wayne smelled like he'd just come from a bar, the odor being one of a mixture of cheap alcohol and stale cigarette smoke. A receding head of lank, greasy hair that needed to be cut curled up on the collar of a leather jacket that looked like it had been expensive, but now it just looked like it had seen better days.

"My favorite niece let me in," Wayne said, staggering across the room to Cassie. He held out his arms and stumbled into her, almost knocking Cassie off of her stool. He righted himself and grabbed Cassie's slender shoulders, leaning into her face in an attempt to kiss her. Cassie recoiled, and Wayne ended up kissing the side of her ear.

"Terrible news about Johnny," Wayne slurred. "Came as soon as I could."

"Thank you," Cassie said, her manners impeccable, as always. "Wayne, this is my friend DeeDee. You spoke on the phone with her the other night. DeeDee, this is Johnny's brother, Wayne."

"Pleased to meet you, Wayne." DeeDee said as she shook Wayne's hand, resisting the urge to rub her palm on the side of her sweater afterwards.

"Where is it?" Wayne said, looking around. "I told you to have it ready."

Cassie sighed. "If you mean the trust fund paperwork, Wayne, I already told you about it. I'm sorry, but I don't know where it is. I'm sure I can find it for you in the next couple of days, but right now I need to take care of more pressing matters."

Wayne's smarmy smile turned into a sneer. He started shaking his finger at Cassie. "I've just about had enough of your scheming and conniving. You know full well where it is. Bet you think you can control me by not giving it to me, just like Johnny did, don't you?" Still shaking, he balled his hands into fists.

Cassie straightened her back and glared at him. "Not at all. I still have a few people to call about the funeral tomorrow. It's a small gathering by invitation only. Some of the people don't even know Johnny's dead. I'll deal with your trust fund information as soon as the funeral is over. You have my word."

Wayne shook his fist in front of Cassie's face. "You must think I'm stupid. If I don't get my money now, I'll…"

Cassie reached up and pushed his hand away. "You'll what, Wayne, hit me?" Her eyes were blazing, daring him to try. "I'm not afraid of you. You're pathetic. Have you looked in a mirror lately? Or had a shower? Your personal hygiene leaves a lot to be desired. If you plan to come to the funeral tomorrow, and you are welcome to, please show some respect for Johnny and clean yourself up."

"Don't talk to me about respect," Wayne yelled. "Johnny never showed me the respect I deserve, and you think you can push me around just like he did. You'll regret this, mark my words, just like Johnny did."

Balto growled at Wayne and started towards him. DeeDee, surprised by the growl, put her hand on the dog to quiet him. It was obvious Cassie had the situation under control and didn't need Balto's help.

Cassie stood up and pushed the stool back. She raised herself up to her full height, which was well below Wayne's shoulders, and pushed him in the chest. "Get out of my house, Wayne, and don't ever come back. You can call my lawyer or do whatever you need to do, but we are done here, am I making myself clear?"

Wayne, silenced by Cassie's outburst, retreated from the kitchen, throwing a few choice insults over his shoulder when he was at a safe enough distance. Cassie and DeeDee heard the heavy front door slam as he left the house.

DeeDee looked at Cassie in amazement, not believing what she'd just witnessed. Cassie was shaking with anger and grief.

"I've got you," DeeDee said, helping Cassie sit back on the stool. "Why don't you let me make those calls you mentioned to tell people about the funeral, and I can also make a pot of coffee for us."

Cassie nodded. "I'd really appreciate it. Thanks, DeeDee. I've got a list of names somewhere around here. It'll take me a minute to find it, but would you mind if I go lie down instead of having coffee? I didn't sleep much last night." She first looked on the kitchen counter and then reached into the back pocket of her jeans, pulling out a crumpled sheet of paper which she handed to DeeDee.

DeeDee smiled. She knew if Cassie was up to making a list, that was a good sign. "You go right ahead. I'll take care of this."

*****

"I don't like the sound of this at all," Jake said when he called DeeDee later in the afternoon. DeeDee had told him about Wayne's visit, and the anger and threats that Johnny's brother had made. "No, I don't like it one bit. Tell me again what exactly he said."

DeeDee tried to remember. "He said something about how Cassie would regret not giving him access to the money. Then he said, and I don't remember his exact words, so I'll paraphrase it, 'Just like Johnny regretted it.'"

With that, Jake sprang into action. "Okay, I think you should stay there tonight with Cassie. I'm going to catch the next ferry to Seattle and come over to Mercer Island as well. Do you think that will be okay with her?"

"Yes, it should be," DeeDee said. "I already told her I brought dinner, and that I'd be happy to stay overnight. Briana and Liam were here earlier, and they'll be back in the morning. Cassie's upstairs resting right now, but I'll speak to her before you get here."

"Okay," Jake said. "DeeDee, there's one more thing I need to tell you." He lowered his voice. "And don't say anything to Cassie about this, all right?"

DeeDee gulped, wondering what was coming. "Uh-huh."

"Don't be alarmed, but Rob was able to get one of our contacts into Wayne's apartment today, when he was at Cassie's. One of the neighbors let him in."

Don't be alarmed? thought DeeDee. *That was Jake's investigator speak for 'Be afraid, be very afraid.'*

DeeDee clutched her cell phone while Jake told her how they'd discovered that Wayne, or someone connected with Wayne, had used his laptop computer to search for information about ricin, a deadly type of poison.

"Is that the type of poison that killed Johnny?" DeeDee whispered.

"Possibly," Jake said, "but it's not certain. Like I told you earlier, Inspector Stewart is here in Seattle, as he's been staking out Greg. He's going to speak to the Seattle police about getting a warrant for Wayne's arrest. I'll be at Cassie's house with my dog, Yukon, as soon as I can. In the meantime, I want you to stay calm, and sit tight. Got it?"

DeeDee heard Cassie coming down the stairs.

"Got it," she said, and ended the call.

CHAPTER TWENTY

DeeDee mentioned to Cassie that Jake was planning on joining them with his dog, Yukon. She didn't want to alarm Cassie, so she kept it vague, saying something about he was worried there might be a problem with the ferry the following day, and he wanted to make sure he'd be able to attend the funeral.

"I'll make dinner, and then you can get to bed nice and early," she suggested. "There's no getting around it, tomorrow's going to be a tough day for you. Are you sure you don't mind if Jake and Yukon come over and spend the night?"

"Of course, I don't mind," Cassie assured her. "It will be nice to have company to keep my mind off everything, and I certainly didn't have a chance to meet Jake properly in Whistler. I'd like to talk to him and get to know him. I can't thank both of you enough, you know, for everything you've done." Once again, her eyes were shining with unshed tears.

"Don't even mention it," DeeDee said. "There is something else I want to talk to you about. I don't think I should go to the funeral tomorrow. You said it was only your closest circle of friends and family, and I didn't bring anything appropriate to wear. I'll stay here and look after the house. I've heard that criminals sometimes check the obituaries and then break into the decedent's home while the family is attending the funeral. Have you ever heard that?"

Cassie nodded. "Yes, but one of the neighbors has already offered to stay at the house, and you must come tomorrow, DeeDee. You're one of my dearest friends. If you need something to wear, there's a closet full of clothes upstairs that belongs to my sister who lives in England. She keeps them for when she comes here on extended visits. She's about your size, so help yourself to whatever you need."

"If you're sure, I ..."

Cassie gave her a warning look

DeeDee nodded. "I will, thank you."

"Good, I'm glad that's settled," Cassie said with a smile. She turned at the sound of the phone ringing in the hallway. "It hasn't stopped all day. I had no idea Johnny knew so many people."

While Cassie excused herself to take the phone call, DeeDee looked in the kitchen cabinets. She'd remembered how Cassie loved Mexican food, and she found rice, beans, and some tortillas, which she'd been pretty sure Cassie would have on hand.

"Okay, that takes care of dinner, Balto. Let's go upstairs and find something to wear."

By the time Jake arrived with Yukon a couple of hours later, DeeDee had prepped dinner and selected a suitable outfit of a gray lightweight silk sweater and matching slacks to wear the following day. She was pleased to discover that Cassie's sister, Beth, also wore the same size shoe as she did, so she'd be able to substitute her stained and well-worn flats for a pair of heels.

DeeDee greeted Jake in the hallway with a kiss.

"Hey, I missed you," he said, pulling her close.

"I'm so happy you're here," she told him quietly. "Cassie doesn't suspect anything might be wrong, but I've been nervous ever since you called. Balto even senses it, he's on high alert, which is very unlike him."

Balto had followed DeeDee into the hallway. His ears pricked up at the mention of his name.

"What are you two lovebirds whispering about?" Cassie asked as she stood in the kitchen doorway.

"Nothing," DeeDee said sheepishly. She turned to the dogs and slapped the side of her thigh. "Balto, Yukon, let's go outside." The dogs, who had been part of the same litter that Jake had brought from Alaska, followed DeeDee out to Cassie's backyard. When she returned, Cassie and Jake were sitting at the kitchen island.

DeeDee sat down beside Jake, who was bringing Cassie up to date on what he'd found out about Wayne. "I told Inspector Stewart about your visit from Wayne today," Jake said, "but it's unlikely the Seattle police will say that's grounds enough for an arrest." He sighed, rubbing his unshaven chin. "I'm sure Wayne's our man, but without anything concrete to go on, there's nothing we can do. I'm sure something will come up in the next couple of days."

DeeDee looked at Jake. He was uncharacteristically somber, and she'd never seen him look so worried. She felt bad about what she'd done earlier. She was pretty certain that going to see Mimi and Derek without telling him had added to his concern.

Cassie suddenly spoke up. "I just remembered something."

DeeDee and Jake watched while she started rooting through her leather purse which was sitting on the countertop. She took out a black phone with a cracked screen and held it up with a sad smile.

"It's Johnny's phone. It must have gotten cracked when he fell." She set it on the countertop. "When the children and I were at the Seattle mortuary today making some last-minute decisions, the funeral director gave it to me. He said the police in Whistler had copied whatever they needed from it and thought I might want it."

"Have you looked at it yet?" Jake asked. "There might be something on it."

Cassie shook her head. "I've been too busy, and quite honestly, I totally forgot about it. Here," she said, pushing it across the counter to Jake. "I have no idea how to use Johnny's phone. He loved gadgets, but I can never figure them out. Do you know how to work it?"

Jake was already tapping and scrolling through the device. DeeDee got up to do the last-minute dinner preparations, and Cassie set the table. After a few minutes studying the phone, Jake slapped the counter. "I knew it," he said, looking up at Cassie.

Both women stopped what they were doing.

"Cassie, I thought you told DeeDee that Johnny was meeting Greg Baker for coffee the morning he died, is that right?"

Cassie nodded. "Yes. He told me about it when we spoke the night before. We even argued about it. It's the last conversation I had with Johnny, so it's burned in my memory. Why?"

"There's nothing here to indicate that Johnny met Greg that morning," Jake said, setting the phone down. "But in his calendar, it shows he was meeting Wayne for coffee."

DeeDee and Cassie shared a look of surprise.

Jake continued talking. "Next to that, there's a notation where Johnny wrote *Interesting. Surprised he could afford to get here.*'" He looked up at the two women. "If Wayne had coffee with Johnny, he could have laced his drink with the ricin poison he'd been researching on his computer. I'm going to call Inspector Stewart right now," Jake said, standing up. "And I'll send the photo we took from Wayne's Facebook page to the Wildflower Restaurant in the hotel to see if anyone working in the restaurant can ID him as being with Johnny that morning."

DeeDee took charge of dinner while Jake went out to make the call to Inspector Stewart. "You sit down, Cassie, and I'll bring everything over to the table," she said. She thought Cassie was looking shaky again, and was relieved to see that Jake was smiling when he returned.

"Good news." Jake said. "Inspector Stewart thinks that might be enough evidence to arrest Wayne, and he hopes Wayne will have the sense to confess. They're going to set up a stakeout at Wayne's apartment. I told Rob to call the Inspector directly with anything he finds out from the hotel, rather than call me first. So, what's for dinner, DeeDee? Something smells delicious."

"It's tortillas with a south of the border style beef," DeeDee said, bringing the warmed-up plates over to the table and sitting down. The serving dishes were laid out in the middle of it. "I made it once before for a dinner party when I was living on Mercer Island. I had a little time last week, so I cooked one and froze it. When I got Cassie's call and decided to spend the night, I brought it with me. She had all the things that go with it."

The talk turned to food, a subject DeeDee was much more comfortable with than murder. "I hope Deelish gets some calls for next year's Cinco de Mayo celebration. Do you think something like this would work for it?"

"Mmm," Jake said, reaching for another tortilla. "Not sure, I'd better test another one just to check."

Cassie laughed, and DeeDee continued. "I could get a piñata filled with Mexican chocolates and have the adults feel like kids when they strike it. Could be a lot of fun."

"That, I like," Jake said, leaning back. "I'll volunteer to fill the piñatas."

DeeDee flushed, stealing a glance at Jake, who winked across the table at her. May was quite a few months away, and Jake was obviously planning on still being around then.

DeeDee was surprised by the amount of food Cassie managed to consume. "That was wonderful," Cassie said. "I didn't think I'd ever be able to eat again, but it really tasted good, plus I need my strength for tomorrow."

"Yes," DeeDee agreed. She was full of sympathy for Cassie. She couldn't imagine what it must be like for her, and she knew her friend was dreading the following day. "Jake and I will clean up the dishes, Cassie. You sit there and don't move, okay?"

"I don't think I could anyway," Cassie said, allowing herself a small smile.

Jake's phone rang just when they had finished cleaning up the kitchen. "Hello, Inspector Stewart," he said, striding out into the hallway.

"Uh-huh," DeeDee could hear him say. "That sounds good, thank you. We will, sir. Good night."

Jake came back and relayed what Inspector Stewart had just told him. "They're watching Wayne's place and want to see what he does next before they arrest him. The more evidence they can get on him, the better chance the arrest has of sticking and of extraditing him to British Columbia for trial."

He turned to Cassie and said, "Rob called him and told him they've got a positive ID on Wayne sitting at a restaurant table with Johnny at the Fairmont the morning Johnny died. There's so much circumstantial evidence, I'd say a tipping point is imminent. Hopefully, this will all be over soon."

Cassie stood up and walked over to Jake. "I hope you're right," she said softly, touching his arm. "But I need to forget all about for now. I'm going to call it a night. There are plenty of bedrooms upstairs for you two, so feel free to take your pick."

She kissed DeeDee on the cheek. "Good night, and thanks again to both of you."

"I'm going to stay downstairs with Yukon on the couch tonight," Jake said after Cassie had left. "I'd feel better if you and Cassie are safe upstairs."

DeeDee hesitated. "What do you think will happen? Did Inspector Stewart say something else?" She wasn't sure if Jake was telling her the whole story.

"Nothing," Jake tried to assure her. "Break-ins are more likely when word gets out about a death in the family, since crooks think the house might be empty, or the family will be too grief-stricken to do anything. I also think Balto and Yukon should stay in the house tomorrow during the funeral for that reason."

"Well..." DeeDee said. She was unable to read Jake's face. "I suppose you're right. I said something like that to Cassie earlier. I'll see you in the morning. Try to get some sleep, okay? Good night."

"I will," Jake promised her, kissing her goodnight.

DeeDee turned to leave, but Balto stayed.

"Balto, go upstairs with DeeDee," Jake commanded.

Balto didn't move.

"I think he wants to stand guard with Yukon. Go upstairs, Balto," Jake said, pointing to the stairs. "Don't think I don't know how you sleep on DeeDee's bed."

Balto looked at DeeDee, and DeeDee looked at Jake, who was trying to keep a straight face.

"I think we'd better get out of here and go upstairs, Balto," DeeDee said.

She knew that every dog trainer would tell her it was stupid to allow it, but Balto had slept at the end of her bed ever since the first night she'd brought him home. Upstairs, she took the bedspread off the bed, folded it, and put it on the chair, so it would be free from dog hair. As soon as she'd brushed her teeth, changed and settled under the covers, Balto jumped up on the bed to take up his usual spot at her feet.

Sometime later DeeDee woke up when she heard a low, deep growl coming from Balto.

"Shhh," she mumbled, sitting up and leaning over to soothe him by stroking his back. What she felt caused her to wake up fully. Balto's guard hairs, the rough hairs along his back, were standing on end. She knew from one of Jake's safety talks that if she ever saw that on Balto, she was to be very, very careful. Jake had told her it was the result of Balto feeling there was a threat to one of them.

DeeDee watched as Balto hopped off the bed and walked over to the door. He looked back at her, waiting for her to get up and follow him. She slipped out of bed, tip-toed across the room, and opened the door. She was unable to hear or see anything in the darkness. She'd taken a few steps down the hall and was standing at the top of the stairs when she froze at the sound of the lock on the front door being rattled. Her heart began to race and her legs felt like they'd turned to jelly. DeeDee started to make her way down the stairs, clutching the stair railing for support. Just then there was the sound of a gunshot and the lock on the door shattered. The door flew open, and Wayne burst into the house, a gun in his hand.

Wayne started randomly shooting and yelling for Cassie. "Get those papers now, hear me?" he roared. "If you don't get them I'm going to enjoy killing you. I've got plenty of ammo, so if you don't give 'em to me, I'll riddle you with hot lead."

The pops from his gun were followed by crashing and the sound of breaking glass. Everything that happened in the next minute or so was a complete blur to DeeDee. Crouched in the darkness with Balto at her side, she waited, certain they were going to die. She was aware of Jake yelling at Wayne to drop his gun, but Wayne continued shooting, hitting furniture and shattering lamps. She thought she saw a dark shadow leap in the direction of the gunfire. There was more yelling that sounded like it was coming from outside the house, and more guns were fired. The smell of cordite from the gunshots filled the air, and it was only when she heard Jake's voice shout that the danger was over did she dare to move.

"Stop, the house is secured!" he yelled. "Don't shoot. This is Jake Rodgers. My dog and I have subdued the suspect. You can come in and get him."

Downstairs, police swarmed throughout the hallway, the house, and the front yard. DeeDee could see Wayne being restrained by police officers. His gun was seized as evidence, and when he was searched, a small plastic baggie containing some white powder was also removed from his person.

"I think if you get that analyzed, you'll find it's ricin," Jake said to Inspector Stewart. "That's the poison I'm certain the coroner will say was the cause of Johnny Roberts' death."

"We will be locking him up in the county jail for now," Inspector Stewart said. "I need to call my department and put in a request for him to be extradited to British Columbia to face murder charges in connection with the death of Johnny Roberts. I think we have a good chance of getting a confession from him tonight, considering the state he's in. I'll be in touch." He shook hands with Jake and nodded to DeeDee who was walking towards them.

Jake placed his arm around DeeDee, and they watched in silence as the police took Wayne away.

"What's going on?" said a sleepy voice behind them belonging to Cassie. "I thought I heard something." As she saw the mess all around her, she held onto the wall for support. "I took a sleeping pill, and thought it was a dream. I could hear Wayne, and there were gunshots."

"It wasn't a dream, Cassie," DeeDee sighed, as she led her into the kitchen to explain that Wayne, Johnny's killer, had just paid them a visit intending to kill Cassie as well.

EPILOGUE

Jake reached out and clasped DeeDee's hand. They were sitting on the deck of her home on Bainbridge Island, quietly looking out at Puget Sound.

"I thought the funeral service was handled well today," Jake said. "The eulogies by Johnny's children were very moving. They were tough to hear and probably even tougher for them to deliver. I wish I'd known Johnny. He sounded like quite a man."

A reflective DeeDee glanced down at her fingers, interlaced with Jake's. "He was," she agreed. "I'm worried about Cassie. She's never been by herself, and I wonder whether she's going to want to stay in that big house on Mercer Island without Johnny. I know how hard it is to have to move away from where you've lived most of your married life. There are so many memories wrapped up in a house like that."

"I don't think she is planning on staying there," Jake said. "We spoke after the service, and she told me that the house is too big for just her. Evidently Johnny left her very well off from the investments he made over the years, and the Mercedes dealership is worth a great deal of money. She's planning on buying a smaller place on Mercer Island, and going back to work at the museum."

DeeDee's gaze followed a flock of birds flying through the pink haze created by the setting sun. "I can understand her wanting to keep busy. She has to go on with life as best she can," she said. "I still can't believe Wayne was the one who killed his brother. I thought it might have been Greg, after what Cassie told us. I hope Greg doesn't get any ideas in his head now that Johnny's dead."

Jake smiled. "Cassie might meet someone else who makes her happy. You did." He squeezed her hand. "Inspector Stewart told me that Wayne has made a full confession. He also had one of his men speak to Greg and ask him where he was on the morning Johnny died. Greg told them Johnny had called him and said that his brother needed to see him urgently. Johnny told Greg he'd have to take a rain check on breakfast."

"Maybe Greg was out to get Johnny as well," DeeDee mused, "but Wayne got there first."

Jake shook his head. "I don't think so. Greg told the Inspector's man that he'd been thinking about what a waste it had been, both Johnny and Greg hating each other the past twenty years. Evidently, he'd told Johnny he'd like to see it end, and Johnny agreed."

"That was big of Johnny," DeeDee said. "Generous to the end." Balto padded over to sit next to DeeDee's feet, and she bent down to pet him.

"By the way, what did you decide to do about that Mercedes you told Mimi you wanted to buy?" Jake was smirking now, and DeeDee raised an eyebrow.

"I could never afford a car like that, not when I'm in the middle of trying to get a new business off the ground, and even if I could, I don't know if I would want it. However, I would be happy with some of the jewelry she was wearing. It gave a new definition to the word 'bling'."

"Hmm, it's not that long till Christmas," Jake said with a wink. "Better be on your best behavior until then."

"Speaking of the holidays," DeeDee said. "I finally got to the bottom of what was going on with Roz. Remember I was worried that she wasn't telling me something?"

Jake nodded. "Is everything okay?"

DeeDee's face broke into a broad smile. "It's more than okay. She and Clark are getting married. My baby sister is settling down at last. The wedding is going to be in Seattle over the holidays, and she asked me to help with the planning since she'll still be in Whistler before the wedding. What do you think?"

Jake leaned over and tucked a strand of hair behind DeeDee's ear. His lips were hovering just above hers.

"I think," he said lifting her hand that he was holding and kissing the back of it, "that Clark is the second luckiest man in the world."

RECIPES

WARM OLIVES
Ingredients:
2 cups assorted olives, your choice (I like to have at l-east three different kinds.)
¼ cup virgin olive oil
1 tsp. fresh ground pepper
6 cloves of garlic, papery covering removed and slivered

Directions:
Preheat oven to 375 degrees. Line a baking sheet with aluminum foil. In a large bowl, combine all the ingredients until well blended. Transfer to the baking sheet and bake until heated through, about 20 minutes. Cool, cover, and refrigerate. Prior to serving, let them come to room temperature. Enjoy!

NOTE: These will keep in the refrigerator for up to one week.

SOUTH OF THE BORDER SLOW COOKED BEEF
Ingredients:
1 tbsp. vegetable oil
3 lb. boneless beef chuck roast

½ tsp. ground cumin
1 tsp. Kosher salt
¼ tsp. freshly ground pepper
16 oz. jar salsa verde
1 white onion, thinly sliced
2 garlic cloves, smashed
Flour tortillas (However many needed for two per person.)
Optional: Shredded cheese, pinto beans, chopped tomatoes,
cilantro served on the side.

Directions:
Heat the vegetable oil in a large skillet over medium-high heat. Season with cumin, salt and pepper. Brown the meat on all sides, approximately 3 minutes per side. Transfer the meat into a 6-quart slow cooker. Add the salsa, onion, and garlic. Cover and cook on high for 6 hours.

Wrap the tortillas in aluminum foil and warm in the oven for about ten minutes. Remove the meat, shred, and serve with tortillas and the optional sides.

NOTE: This can be made ahead and frozen. Put it in a large pan and warm on the stovetop over medium-low heat.

CHOCOLATE TIRAMISU CAKE
NOTE: This is best when made 2 – 3 days in advance. Yes, I know the recipe looks intimidating, but trust me, it's worth it.

Ingredients:
Cake:
2 cups sugar
1 ¾ cups all-purpose flour
1 ½ tsp. baking powder
1 ½ tsp. baking soda
¼ cup cocoa powder
1 tsp. fine salt
1 cup milk (whole)

2 large eggs, lightly beaten (I prefer jumbo.)
½ cup vegetable oil
2 tsp. vanilla extract (Don't use imitation. If you're going to take the time to make something this fabulous, don't ruin it by not using the real thing.)
1 cup boiling water
Cooking spray
2 tbsp. flour (For dusting the cake pans.)
2 cake pans (Mine have an 8 ½" diameter.)
Parchment paper (If you don't have it on hand, you can use aluminum foil or even plastic wrap.)
Springform pan (Mine has a 9 ½" diameter. It gives me a little "wiggle room.")

Brushing Liquid:
¾ cup brewed coffee
¼ cup dark crème de cacao or Kahlua liqueur

Mascarpone Filling:
2 ½ cups mascarpone cheese
½ cup sugar
¼ to ½ cup heavy cream
¼ tsp. ground cinnamon

Dusting Mixture:
½ cup unsweetened cocoa powder
1 cup powdered sugar

Directions:
Cake:
Preheat the oven to 350 degrees. Prepare cake pans by spraying with nonstick spray and lightly dusting with flour. Whisk the sugar, flour, cocoa, baking powder, baking soda, and salt together. Stir in eggs, milk, oil, and vanilla.

Beat with an electric mixer on medium speed for 2 minutes. Stir in boiling water and mix until blended. Divide the mixture in half and pour equal amounts into cake pans which have been sprayed with the cooking spray. Bake until a wooden skewer inserted into the middle of the cake comes out clean, approximately 30 to 35 minutes. Put the pans on a wire rack and let cool.

When cool, remove from cake pans and split each one horizontally in half with a serrated knife, so you wind up with four cake layers. (I found the easiest way to do this is to put the cake on a piece of parchment paper.

Take a serrated knife and score it halfway down from the top. Keep turning the parchment paper until the cake has been completely scored, then using the scored marks as a guide, cut it in half.)

Brushing Liquid:
Combine the coffee and the liqueur.

Filling:
In a large bowl beat the cheese, ¼ cup of coffee mixture, sugar, ¼ cup of cream, and the cinnamon until smooth. If the mixture appears to be too thick, thin it down with the extra cream as needed.

Assembly:
Place a layer of the cake in the springform pan. Brush the cake with ¼ of the remaining brushing liquid and spread ¼ of mascarpone mixture on it. Repeat the process, ending with a fourth cake layer. Brush with remaining brushing liquid and spread the remaining the mascarpone mixture on the top layer.

When ready to serve, remove the springform pan sides, combine the dusting mixture, and lightly dust the top using a sieve. Enjoy!

PEAR AND GRUYERE SALAD WITH HONEY-DIJON MUSTARD DRESSING

Ingredients:
Dressing:
1 cup vegetable oil

½ cup rice vinegar

2 tbsp. Dijon mustard

2 tsp. honey

1 ½ tsp. salt

½ tsp. cayenne pepper

Directions:

Whisk together all the ingredients until thickened. Can be refrigerated for one week.

Salad
Ingredients:

4 ripe pears, cored and cut into ½" thick wedges, mixed gently with 1 tbsp. fresh lemon juice

½ lb. Gruyere cheese, cut into ½" thick slices (Feel free to substitute a cheese of your choice, as Gruyere can be a bit pricey.)

4 cups seedless red grapes, halved lengthwise

Butter lettuce

Assembly:

Place butter lettuce leaves on serving platter. Alternate the pears and the cheese until the platter is filled. Scatter the grapes over the top. Drizzle the dressing over the salad. Enjoy!

SWEET POTATO AND FONTINA GRATIN
Ingredients:

3 medium sweet potatoes, peeled and sliced into ¼ inch round pieces

2 tbsp. butter

3 tbsp. all-purpose flour

½ cup cream

1 cup shredded Fontina cheese (4 oz.)

1 tbsp. fresh thyme leaves

Freshly ground pepper and salt to taste

Nonstick cooking spray

Directions:

Preheat oven to 350 degrees. Lightly coat a gratin dish or a baking dish with nonstick spray. In a medium saucepan melt the butter over medium heat. Whisk in the flour and cook for 1 minute. Stir in cream and cook until thickened.

Reduce heat to low and add ¾ cup of cheese, stirring until melted. Add thyme, salt, pepper, and gently stir to combine. Place sweet potato slices in baking dish, pour sauce over them, and sprinkle with remaining cheese. Bake, covered, about one hour or until the sweet potatoes are fork-tender. Let stand 15 minutes before serving. Enjoy!

Paperbacks & Ebooks for FREE

Go to www.dianneharman.com/freepaperback.html and get your FREE copies of Dianne's books and favorite recipes immediately by signing up for her newsletter.

Once you've signed up for her newsletter you're eligible to win three paperbacks. One lucky winner is picked every week. Hurry before the offer ends!

ABOUT THE AUTHOR

Dianne lives in Huntington Beach, California, with her husband, Tom, a former California State Senator, and her boxer dog, Kelly. Her passions are cooking, reading, and dogs, so whenever she has a little free time, you can either find her in the kitchen, playing with Kelly in the back yard, or curled up with the latest book she's reading.

Her award winning books include:

Cedar Bay Cozy Mystery Series
Kelly's Koffee Shop, Murder at Jade Cove, White Cloud Retreat, Marriage and Murder, Murder in the Pearl District, Murder in Calico Gold, Murder at the Cooking School, Murder in Cuba, Trouble at the Kennel, Murder on the East Coast, Trouble at the Animal Shelter, Murder & The Movie Star

Liz Lucas Cozy Mystery Series
Murder in Cottage #6, Murder & Brandy Boy, The Death Card, Murder at The Bed & Breakfast, The Blue Butterfly, Murder at the Big T Lodge, Murder in Calistoga

High Desert Cozy Mystery Series
Murder & The Monkey Band, Murder & The Secret Cave, Murdered by Country Music, Murder at the Polo Club

Midwest Cozy Mystery Series
Murdered by Words, Murder at the Clinic

Jack Trout Cozy Mystery Series
Murdered in Argentina

Northwest Cozy Mystery Series
Murder on Bainbridge Island, Murder in Whistler

Coyote Series
Blue Coyote Motel, Coyote in Provence, Cornered Coyote

Midlife Journey Series
Alexis

Website: www.dianneharman.com, **Blog:** www.dianneharman.com/blog
Email: dianne@dianneharman.com

Newsletter

If you would like to be notified of her latest releases please go to www.dianneharman.com and sign up for her newsletter.

Made in United States
Troutdale, OR
07/29/2024